Love notes from
VINEGAR
HOUSE

ALSO BY KAREN TAYLEUR

Six

Hostage

Chasing Boys

The David Mortimore Baxter series

Liar

Excuses

The Truth

Promises

Secrets

Manners

All Stars 2: Bree, Centre

All Stars 7: Mel, Goal Attack

Halloween in Christmas Hills

Our Stories: Burke & Wills

Love notes from VINEGAR HOUSE

Karen Tayleur

black dog books

The author gratefully acknowledges the
support of the May Gibbs
Children's Literature Trust.

First published in 2012
by ✖ **black dog books**
an imprint of Walker Books Australia Pty Ltd
Locked Bag 22, Newtown
NSW 2042 Australia
www.walkerbooks.com.au

National Library of Australia Cataloguing-in-Publication entry:
Tayleur, Karen, 1961–
Love notes from vinegar house / Karen Tayleur.
ISBN: 978 1 742032 19 1 (pbk.)
For young adults
A823.4

Cover image © Marcus Lindstrom/Vetta/Getty Images
Typeset in Garamond
Printed and bound in Australia by Griffin Press

10 9 8 7 6 5 4 3 2 1

For Alex Segulin,
fellow spy, evader of piranha and
Deadly Ernest devotee;
and for those of us who will miss him.

Chapter 1

There are three things you should know about me if we're ever going to be friends. The first thing is my name – Freya Jackson Kramer. Don't bother teasing me about my second name. Luke Hart teased me about it once, and he got a kick in the shin, but I don't need to talk about him and I don't need to discuss my middle name. Obviously, I am a girl. Obviously, my middle name is not a girl's name. It's my mother's maiden name and, well … it's really none of your business at this point but it's usually best to get it out of the way early.

The second thing is that I don't believe in ghosts – not the scary white sheet, boogie-woogie type of ghost anyway. And yet … I don't disbelieve either. I'm kind of sitting on the ghost fence, dangling my legs on both sides, not sure which way to jump. I think I might be here for a while.

And the third thing is that I believe in karma. After I interfered with the love notes at Vinegar House I am due for some payback. But it wasn't something I planned, so that's got to count for something in the karma stakes. There are other things you should probably know about me as well, but those are the three main things: my name, the ghost thing, and the fact that I believe in karma.

I live in a tiny place called Homsea, which is *a delightful seaside village chock-full of interesting antique stores and bookshops, and home to one of the oldest cemeteries in our region*. (This description is from the holiday brochure stuck up on the pinboard at home – I have no idea why it's there.) I know. Fascinating, huh? If you're looking for excitement and glamour and fashion and entertainment, DO NOT VISIT HOMSEA. I love it. It's my home. But Homsea can be a little … what's the word … *boring*. Mind-numbing. Irksome. Tedious. Dull. These are other words that describe Homsea. It's a very describable place.

While Homsea may not be the centre of the universe, I have to admit that it is the centre of mine. I can walk down the main street blindfolded and tell you the name of each shop, the special of the day at Sudholz Meats, and the person serving behind each counter – or sitting as is usually the case with Miss Maudy in the Quilt Barn.

The main street, imaginatively named Main Street, is long and wide, with deep gutters that run like the Homsea River when the rains break the summer dry spell. The shops are ancient. They were mostly built when Homsea was settled in the 1800s, and they crouch low on both sides of the street like our dog, Deefa, when he knows he's in trouble for digging up the garden. The oldest ones are made from stone. Some have verandahs out the front. Mitchell's Bakery even has some chairs and tables, which is where a few of the mums meet after school drop-off in the mornings.

If you take a left at the first crossroad into town off the highway, you will find a two-storey building. It was built by Heinze Gascke, the founding father of Homsea. It used to be his home, but now it's a library. Further down is the police station where Rudy Heinrich spends a lot of time sitting in his car in the driveway facing the road, just waiting for out-of-towners to speed past him. He is a regular visitor to Mitchell's Bakery and can often be seen shoving a pastry into his mouth with one hand while holding his radar gun in the other. He prefers the apricot danish because it contains fruit and this makes it a balanced meal. That's what he told me one day when I was buying a chocolate croissant and he was waiting to be served.

My home isn't close to the shops, it's nearer to the beach. Our house is a nothing kind of house. It's not really old and it's not really new. It's a long narrow building that kicks out at one end where Dad has built on an office so that he can do paperwork when he gets home from his day job. Some of the windows get stuck in summer and there's a creak on the porch where the supporting stump has rotted away. Two summers ago Dad restumped the house himself, but he didn't quite get to the porch, which was the reason for the restumping in the first place. Mum wants to get a builder in to fix it, but Dad keeps promising he'll get around it to it. I wouldn't be holding my breath if I were Mum.

Our long-time neighbours, the Humes, moved to Port Eden a month ago and we're still waiting for the new neighbours to move in. The Humes were looking for a retirement home with more facilities than Homsea could offer. That's what Mrs Hume told me. But Mr Hume told me plainer than that.

"Why would I want to move into a smaller house at Homsea Haven with no garden when I can move to a smaller house with a garden that someone else looks after? And a swimming pool! And free meals and a games room and dancing every Friday night!"

He nearly convinced me to move as well, except as always I was distracted by the way his teeth clacked off his gums every time he opened his mouth. After our discussion, I went home and brushed my teeth for ten minutes straight because he reminded me that I didn't want to end up with false teeth.

Anyway, what I'm saying is, we lose a lot of local people to Port Eden.

For a long while, Homsea was the poor cousin of Port Eden where the buildings are newer and the multiplex cinema shows the nearly-latest films. Then the Homsea traders got the idea to market our town as *A quaint snapshot of yesteryear, filled with antiques and good old-fashioned friendly service.* This welcome sign was created by Porky Sudholz, whose magic way with words was usually restricted to the blackboard specials of the week outside his butcher shop. (*Snag a bargain today! Steak your claim on the best meat in town! Baa-gains galore!*) The trickle of tourists turned into a flood and the rest is history.

There are not many landmarks in Homsea. I've already mentioned the library, popular for its internet access and plush meeting rooms (courtesy of Miss Maudy who has turned them into a mix of *Quilter's Life* magazine meets the Arabian Nights), perfect for book clubs and craft groups. Think old people.

The outdoor cinema, which opens on the first day of summer and closes at the end of autumn, is also popular. Families with young children love to take along blankets and deckchairs and eat fish and chips straight out of the paper wrapping. It's not a good place for making out, because you're just as likely to be sitting next to your fifth grade teacher or the lady from the supermarket who is going to tell your mum. (Just between you and me, this happened to my sister Isabella. Mum thought it was funny, but she didn't tell Dad. There are Things That Dad Needs To Know and this is not one of them.)

Then there's the long splintery jetty that stretches out across the water like a grey pointing finger. Like an exit sign – this way out. Many people are in a hurry to leave Homsea. Maybe they're embarrassed by its quaintness. A lot of my sister's friends have left to go to uni and some of them haven't been back, even for holidays.

In summer, the jetty is a tourist hotspot – no doubt about that. Couples shuffle from one end of the jetty to the other, then back again. Parents hold tightly onto the ice-cream-sticky hands of their kids as they peer over the edge. It's fun to watch the blue swimmer crabs doing the quickstep across the sandy floor. They go sideways, left and right, like they're faking a pass in a basketball game.

At the end of the jetty, which is stained with ink, fishermen dance their squid jigs across the darker blue water – jiggling and swaying their lures. Some of the tourists use the frozen pilchards from the Fish Co-op as bait, but the only thing this gets them is stinking hands that smell of fish and nothing in their bucket. I could have told them that. Teens, mainly boys, hang out underneath the pylons on the beach, smoking and lying to each other about the night before, and spying at girls through the gaps in the grey boards. Teens, mainly girls, hang about the jetty just above the pylons and talk about the boys as if they don't know they're listening in.

A few tourists still brave the jetty in winter, but mainly it's the locals you'll find, fishing lines in the water, woollen hats pulled down over their ears. For years, Luke Hart and I had an understanding that at high tide on Saturday morning we'd meet at the end of the jetty for an hour of serious squiding. Most times we'd hardly say a word, just casting and pulling in our lines at the hint of a tug. Then everything got screwed up …

But I don't want to talk about that.

What I'm saying is that when I'm there, sitting on

the jetty edge, dangling my legs and watching the water chop up into ruffles, I am home. That's where I ended up after school on that last day of term before I went to stay at Vinegar House.

So the winter holidays started out like any other …

No, wait. Strike that.

The winter holidays began a little differently to the many I'd had before. It's just that I wasn't paying attention at the time.

Chapter 2

That winter, everyone deserted me. My best friend, Holly, my sister, Isabella, and my little brother, Oscar, were scattered about the map. (Oscar, I didn't miss so much.)

Holly was on a student exchange in Paris – Paris, France that is! Could she have been further away? Winter holidays are always boring, but at least Holly and I are usually bored together. Being bored alone was worse to the power of a thousand.

I was having a fight with friends at school, which meant I was staying off Facebook. It was just this thing that happened at a party … Anyway, I'd already spent five days away from the site, but it was still the first thing I thought of logging on to when I sat down to the computer. I was also screening my calls and texts. There were some messages I didn't even bother to read, depending on who they were from.

Isabella was on a uni break and up north for two

weeks visiting friends. Oscar had signed up for a school holiday camp, though I expected him home at any moment with a bad case of broken-bone-itis. My brother is accident-prone. He knows all the Casualty doctors in Port Eden by their first names. Mum even has her own car parking space right near the front door.

That's one of Mum's jokes.

She's not very funny, but I've never told her that because apart from her lame jokes, she is mainly nice.

The phone call that started it all came through at six o'clock in the morning on the third day of school holidays. I like to count the weekends as part of the holidays – it sounds as if you have more time off – so this made it a Monday. I hate Mondays. Even on holidays. So it was a Monday, and the first thing I thought of when the phone rang, well one of the first things, was Urgh, it's Monday and I felt the weight of Monday hit me like a truckload of frozen bait.

It was Holly's birthday, and I'd been talking to her on the landline the night before (my night, her afternoon or morning – I could never get a handle on the time difference). The cordless phone handset I'd shoved under my pillow was a demented cricket chirping loudly into my ear. My stomach lurched upwards as I was pulled out of a stupid dream where my feet were stuck in sand while waves dumped seaweed over my head. I stabbed blindly at the keypad and finally fluked the talk button.

Let me give you a hint about phone calls that early in the morning – they're not from someone telling you that you've won the lottery or the Nobel Peace Prize. They're not even offering to save you money by introducing you to a new phone plan. My first thought was that it was the camp nurse saying that Oscar needed some minor surgery, but it was Carole, my mother's sister.

"Freya?"

Her voice was tight and so unlike her usual bright, breezy manner that my stomach dropped down to my bedsocks. Then up, then down, a terrifying rollercoaster ride. When Aunt Carole asked for my mother, I stumbled to my parent's room, the fog of sleep clearing with each step. Mum was already sitting up in bed looking alarmed, so I handed her the phone and perched on the end of the bed to listen in.

Look, I don't want to go into details, but my Nanna was very sick. Which was sad, but kind of like finding out that the neighbour who lived down the road – the one who dropped birthday cards and Christmas cards into your letterbox every year – was in hospital. If you looked at a world globe and found where we lived, you'd have to spin it 180 degrees to find out where Nanna lived. I didn't really know her, and she didn't really know me.

Of course, it was different for Mum.

Mum was a mess, rushing around, pulling clothes from drawers, flicking through the filing cabinet for her passport, then stopping to stare off into the distance, slow tears leaking down her cheeks. My mum is the sort of person who usually only cries at movies, never when things were really tough, so it was like watching a stranger impersonating her and not doing a very convincing job. I made Mum a cup of tea, because that's what they did in the movies, and then I sent her outside to sit in the morning sun with the distraction of Deefa going crazy around her feet.

"I'm going to have to go with your mother," Dad said as he strode about.

Let me tell you something about my father; he never walks, or casually saunters, but strides, even if it's only to bed. I call him the Colonel, though never to his face.

"Can you stay at Holly's? I'm not sure how long this is going to take."

"Holly's in France," I reminded him.

18

"Right. Hell, what a mess." He ran his fingers through his brown hair, which was thin on top and showed pink bits of scalp.

"I'll be fine," I said. More than fine, actually, I thought.

Home alone.

Already I was making plans for late, late nights and takeaway dinners. Maybe I could sort the school friends mess out and have a quiet gathering of thirty or so—

"Could you stay with Holly's mother?" he muttered.

"I'm not staying at Holly's without Holly being there," I said.

Seriously. Sometimes it felt like Dad had been born at the age of fifty, which would have been quite uncomfortable for his mother. Even though I had seen photos of him as a teenager, I couldn't imagine him ever worrying about a zit, or getting up the courage to go on a first date, or partying late the night before an exam.

I stood up to look out the window at Mum, who was warming her hands around the teacup and ignoring the dog. Things were obviously bad. She loved that dog.

"I can stay here. I am perfectly old enough to live by myself," I said.

"Don't you have other friends? What's that girl … Barbara?"

"Bridie," I corrected. "And no, everyone's away." Dad didn't have a clue who my friends were or what they were doing. They are also not on my Things That Dad Needs To Know list.

"Maybe I should get Isabella to come home–"

"Dad!"

"Freya, it's out of the question. Money's a bit tight at the moment – we just can't afford to take you with us. And you can't stay here by yourself. How are you going to get about?"

"Dad, I'm on holidays. I don't need to be driven around. I can walk to the supermarket from here."

Even though I usually badgered for a lift if ever I had to go there. I mean, it's only a couple of blocks from home, but it is uphill. More of an incline than hill, really.

"The Dunbars live just down the road if I get stuck," I said.

Even though they were stuck up snobs and they always ignored me whenever I walked past their house. Just because of that embarrassing incident four Halloweens ago … I don't really want to talk about that though.

"What else is there? I've got stacks of homework. I'll just hang out at home, like I'm already doing anyway. What's the difference?" I didn't mention the Harts, our neighbours across the road, although once they would have been at the top of my list of friends.

The same moment the idea crossed my mind, Dad said, "I'd ask the Harts, but they've got a houseful of relatives."

I was glad I couldn't go there.

"So, Dad–" I began.

But the Colonel was already striding out of the room, punching at the numbers of his mobile phone, totally ignoring me as usual. Look out. National emergency. Maybe he was calling the prime minister.

I decided that I would talk to Mum after things had settled down a bit. I had friends who'd lived alone for days at a time. Didn't my parents trust me?

But I never had a chance to talk to Mum about the whole staying at home thing because a half an hour later Dad had some wonderful news. I thought maybe he'd had a call from Aunt Carole to say everything was okay and that Nan's illness was a false alarm. In fact, he had rung Grandma to ask if I could stay with her.

Fffffantastic.

"Your grandmother has a few appointments in Port

Eden next week, but that's only an overnight stay," said Dad.

"Next week?" I repeated.

"Freya, I don't know how long this is going to take," said Dad.

That stopped me in my tracks, because my father knows everything. What did he mean he didn't know how long this was going to take?

"And Rumer will be there, so you two girls can keep each other company," said my father.

Really, really fffffantastic.

Rumer.

My least-favourite cousin.

Chapter 3

Let me tell you about Rumer. I don't want you to think that I go around hating people, because I don't. I have a lot of friends. Well, not a lot, not thousands or anything, but I have many friends and one really good friend – Holly. But I was telling you about Rumer. Rumer and I don't like each other much, but our families insist we are the best of friends. Technically, this is not correct. We are best friends like cats and dogs might be. Or like oil and water. Or like a glass of milk and someone with lactose intolerance. You get the idea. Rumer is older than me, but it is only a two-year gap. If only the gap between the rest of our lives wasn't five billion light-years apart. Still, Rumer wasn't too bad – just as long as I did everything she wanted.

I don't know about you, but I hate bossy people.

When we were younger, Rumer always made up games where the rules shifted depending on how she was feeling. This made trying to win pretty impossible.

And Rumer was always the hero. My roles ranged from weakling foe to snivelling servant and even unloved pet. If Rumer was the star of the show, I was like one of those actors in the credits way down near the gaffer boy. Or maybe just stunt girl number two.

Once, at Grandma's house, I was given the role of wild dog suffering from rabies. Not one of my finest moments. I figured if I got too tired of the game I could bite Rumer on the leg and blame it on losing myself in the character. I never got a chance to bite Rumer, though, because she tied me to a tree then went off and forgot about me. I was stuck shivering under the tree until Isabella came to find me for lunch. I kicked Rumer when I found her. I got into trouble from my parents – she screamed as if I'd tried to kill her – but Grandma gave me a nod and handed me a peppermint. It was so hot I thought it had burned my voice clear out of its box.

There are things I think about sometimes that I usually keep to myself. For instance, have you ever thought about a voice box? I mean, can it really be a box? And if it's not a box, then why not call it something else? Like a voice cube? Or a voice oval? I've tried feeling my neck for my voice box, but found nothing even vaguely resembling a square shape.

Luke Hart has an Adam's apple that goes up and down on his neck when he speaks. But that's not a box. Doesn't really look much like an apple either. And the strange thing is, one day it just appeared. From out of nowhere. He went from having a smooth neck to one with a bobbing thing that did not resemble an apple at all.

Anyway, how did you get me talking about Luke Hart?

I was talking about Rumer and how incredibly annoying she is. The only person who doesn't give in to Rumer is Grandma.

Grandma lives in a rambling old double-storey house that has three names. The locals call it Kramer's Folly. Kramer is my grandmother's last name. It's my last name too, but I already told you that. The house's official name, the one on the brass nameplate near the front doors, is Burnside. And the cousins call it Vinegar House, after Grandma Vinegar – not her real name of course.

Sometimes I dream about Vinegar House. It starts with the smell of lavender. None of my dreams ever make sense, and this one's no different. First there's the smell. Then I find myself in the suffocating stillness of the Blue Room. This is the official name for the blue bedroom upstairs. It's pitch-black – no wait, that's a cliché. We studied clichés in English last year. It's Wild Child's Incredibly Black Mascara black – the kind that doesn't run, even if you cry. I only know I'm in the Blue Room because of the texture of the blackness. I'll explain about that later. So I'm trapped in a hiding space. I hear heavy breathing that isn't mine. Silent screams choke my throat, and my skin crawls like it's trying to leave my bones and find another home. (Hey, see ya, skin. Bye. No, really, thanks for staying with me for so long.)

And then, somehow – dreams do not have to make sense – I am downstairs in the entry hall, staring up at the main staircase looking like it belongs in a giant's castle. I walk slowly up the stairs that crumble behind me.

I don't want to go to the Blue Room. But I'm like one of those people you see in a scary movie – you know, the kind of movie where you yell at the actor for doing something stupid like walking into danger. (Look behind you! Don't go in there! Can't you hear the scary music?)

Still, it's like I have no choice. I'm moving like I'm following a script.

(*Actor walks up staircase.*)

26

Ragged curtains flap out a warning from the broken stairwell windowpanes.

(*Actor ignores flapping ragged curtains.*)

I know that Grandma's going to be cross about the broken windows, but there's no time to stop and clean it up.

(*Actor is obviously out of her mind.*)

And the strange thing is that the staircase just gets longer and steeper at every twist and turn, until I have to drag myself up each step like a rock climber. Then the handrail crumbles beneath my hand and I am falling, spinning in space until I jolt awake.

If I had a choice between being stuck in wet sand and climbing the stairs at Vinegar House, I'd choose the sand every time. Of course, I'd rather not have any nightmares at all, but you don't always get to choose what you want.

Including your relatives.

My great-great-grandfather, Willem Kramer, had been born into family money, and he splashed his wealth about like a kid in the shallows at the Homsea foreshore. He was famous for losing the family fortune, then making his own when there was nothing left to spend. Great-great Grandpa showed off his new wealth by building his dream home. Unfortunately, he

chose the most ridiculous site for his grand house –
for it was built in the middle of the end of nowhere,
on the edge of a ragged bluff. It stands on a slight
lean so that it always looks in danger of falling into
the sea, though Uncle Stephen says that the lean is just
an illusion – something to do with the tilt of the land.
Uncle Stephen is a very smart man, so he is probably
right. Sometimes, when I look at the house, it's like a
huge monster leaning over to devour me. And then
in a blink it just looks like a normal old house. The
house plays tricks like that. It's not a friendly house.
Everyone in Homsea thinks it is cursed.

The house itself was built in the late 1800s. A row
of stables and a small groundskeeper's cottage, further
up the hill, was added some time after that. A triple-car
garage was built behind the stables in the 1950s by my
grandpa, but you can't see it from the house.

I've seen photographs from the 1920s of "the staff"
lined up with the grand house as a backdrop, looming
over them. About that time, two of the maids died in
a fire that started in the outhouse laundry. Around the
same time, one of the stable hands died when he was
thrown from a horse that Great-great Grandpa had
won in a bet. I'd also heard a whisper of a drowning
near Seal Rock, just off Bluff Beach. Perhaps that's

where the idea of the house being cursed came from.

By the time I was born, Grandma Vinegar (her real name is Florence) had been a widow of twenty years, and was what my mother called "careful with her money". Others just called her mean. Her grandchildren secretly called her Grandma Vinegar due to her sharp and bitter tongue. No one was safe from it – not even the adults. Of course we never called her Grandma Vinegar to her face, but Isabella insisted that Grandma had somehow found out our secret name and seemed happy about it. The only softness I ever saw in Grandma was when she stroked her cats, Nutmeg and Cinnamon. Lucky *she* fussed over them, for they were the oldest and mangiest felines on the planet, and no one else cared. I think they shared two teeth between them.

I hope you're not a cat lover.

I love cats.

Just not those cats.

I think Grandma loved those cats better than any human. She always referred to Grandpa Theo as dear Theo in a dry way so that I was never sure if she missed him or mocked him. A large oil painting of Grandpa Theo, set in a heavy frame, reminded us of his absence every time we visited Vinegar House. It was painted by a semi-famous artist and had won a prize when Dad was a teenager. Grandma said it was a good likeness of her husband, though the suit hid the wide set of his shoulders and the huge expanse of his chest. Isabella and I agreed that what Grandma really meant was that he was fat. It was strange to think of my grandfather being so big, as my grandmother was a dry twig, withering with age. I often wondered how they looked together.

I am taller than Grandma, by at least a head, but she has this way of making you feel small. Everyone says that I am going to be tall like my dad, but I guess he got his height from his dad. I am shorter than Luke Hart, but not too short that I couldn't stand on my tiptoes and kiss him straight on the mouth …

I was talking about my grandfather.

The painting of Grandpa Theo sits above the marble fireplace in the drawing room. No one else I know has a drawing room, and when I was younger I used to think Grandma called it that because of the many paintings on the walls. Which should have made it the painting room, I suppose. Grandma always dressed as though visitors might drop in at any moment, but I never met any of her friends. Usually, it was just the family; Mrs Skelton, the cook-come-cleaner; and Mr Chilvers, the gardener-come-handyman at the house. Grandma did sometimes talk about the girls in Port Eden whose average age would have been eighty not out.

Don't get me wrong. I like old people. But eighty is not the age of a girl. I'm very fussy about using the right words for things. Except for the word "death".

The drawing room is where we hand out the Christmas presents every year. Just once I would like a Christmas day at our house, but all the important events on our family calendar happen at Vinegar House. We gather there on special occasions such as Christmas or birthdays, or even just ordinary occasions, when Grandma decides she needs the family about her. The gatherings are a great time to catch up with the cousins.

We used to play games like Spotlight or Spies (our very own special game) or Murder in the Dark when we were younger. And there were always board games. There wasn't much else to do at Vinegar House. Grandma believes that unless children are doing chores (this is where you do work for no money) then they should use their imaginations (this means all TV watching, laptops and electronic games are banned). Mobile phone coverage at Vinegar House is touch and go, but that isn't usually an issue as all mobiles are checked at the hallstand in the entry.

Like the United Nations, I'm guessing.

Or a really strict trivia night at the Homsea Town Hall.

This used to cause fury in my older sister Isabella, who said it was like living in a police state. She stopped trying to sneak her phone into Vinegar House after Grandma threw my cousin Lee's mobile through the open dining room double doors when it rang during one of her dinner parties. (Lee and I found it later in the azalea bushes after everyone had moved into the drawing room for cake.) Even the adults turn their mobiles off. The only one who doesn't is Uncle Stephen because he is a doctor and is very important.

Murder in the Dark was a favourite game of the cousins, but it was only fun when there were more than three players. Rumer was always in charge of the rules. She ordered us about and acted like she was years older than everyone else, when in fact she was younger than Isabella, Julia and the twins – Lee and Angus. The first time I played, I had just turned eight. Up until then I had been part of the younger cousins gang that played downstairs under the watchful eye of our parents.

I was very excited to be part of the Blue Room gang that day. I remember it well. It was the day I found out what sort of person my cousin Rumer really was.

Chapter 4

"Lee, guard the door. Are we ready?" demanded Rumer.

It was Grandma Vinegar's birthday, and the whole family had gathered to sing "Happy Birthday", watch her blow out the candles on her cake, and give her presents that she would stick in the bottom of her wardrobe drawer and never use. All the cousins were there, and the younger ones had been seated at the children's table, which was really just a low coffee table covered with a white tablecloth. I was at the adults' table and feeling very pleased with my promotion.

Dinner had gone on forever, and I was sick of trying to remember my table manners, trying to use the right cutlery, and keeping my elbows from popping onto the table as if they had a mind of their own. There was a lot of laughter coming from the kids' table, and they were already up to dessert before we'd even started on our main meal. My cousin Lee and his friend Bryn sat opposite Isabella and me, and spent the whole dinner trying to make Isabella laugh out loud. I got bored with their game and found a tiny hole in the white tablecloth that hung down past my knees and picked away at it making a larger hole until Isabella asked if we could leave the table. Grandma nodded her head once, giving us her permission.

There was a scramble of chairs as we made a beeline to the Blue Room upstairs, away from the adults. For years the Blue Room had been used only as a guest room and the dried lavender on the dressing table couldn't mask its damp mouldy smell – think a wet towel left in the bottom of a swim bag. The room was easily as big as our living room at home, and the ceiling rose so high up that it ended in shadow. Blue floral wallpaper lined the walls. It was a fuzzy kind of wallpaper and it sent a shudder through me whenever I touched it. There were heavy blue velvet drapes on either side of the window. The bed was high off the ground and looked very lumpy, and a hatstand stood in one corner of the room holding an old wool coat and a large straw sunhat. Other dark furniture was pushed up against the walls, including a floor-length, gold-framed mirror and a large armchair.

"Are we allowed here?" I asked.

"Dad's sleeping here," said Rumer, "so I'm sure *I'm* allowed here. And if I've invited you in, then that's okay. You write the notes, Julia," she said in her bossy way.

"Did you say this room was haunted?" asked Bryn.

Angus looked at me quickly then punched Bryn in the arm and told him to be quiet.

Lee kept guard on the door while Julia wrote on a piece of lined paper. She then tore the paper into long thin strips and folded them over so the writing on the paper was covered. Bryn and Angus, Lee's twin brother, pushed each other to see who would fall over first, while Isabella watched them with a little smile.

"Now, do we all know the rules?" asked Rumer.

As usual, Rumer was bossing people around, and it annoyed me so much that I kicked the dressing table. A crystal trinket box fell to the floor with a muffled thud, spilling hairpins, tiny loose pearls and a small key onto the floral carpet.

"Freya! Do you want to play or not?" Rumer stood over me, hands on hips, as I picked the box and its contents up off the floor. Isabella helped me.

"Shut up, Rumer," said Isabella, calmly.

"She always ruins things," said Rumer. "We should have left her with the babies." Rumer sighed theatrically. "She's probably going to cry and tell the adults everything we're doing."

"That's enough, Rumer," said Isabella. "Don't be a pain." Then Isabella looked at me sternly. "Do you promise to cross your throat and hope to choke if you tell any adult about this game?"

I nodded solemnly. Then I decided to kick Rumer instead of the dressing table, but Angus grabbed my shoulders and held me fast as if he could read my mind.

"She's no baby, Ru," he said. "Anyway, it's better with more people. Hurry up."

"I don't get what she's doing," said Bryn.

I'd met Bryn several times at Vinegar House, although I didn't know why he came along with Lee, and I never thought to ask. He seemed nice enough. He was Isabella's age, and I could tell she liked him, because she kept punching him in the arm whenever he teased her.

"Murder in the Dark," said Rumer. "There are seven of us playing, so there are seven strips of paper."

"Yep," said Bryn, seriously.

"A word is written on each piece of paper. Six strips will have the word 'player', and one strip will have the word 'murderer' written on it."

"Finished," said Julia, and she looked about before grabbing the straw hat from the hat stand and shoving the folded strips of paper inside.

"So we all take a strip and read the word," said Rumer, pulling a scrap of paper from the hat. "But you can't tell anybody what note you have—"

"Murderer," read Bryn, laughing loudly as he read his note.

Lee groaned. "You don't tell anyone, idiot."

I thought Rumer would get cross, but instead she laughed a little and said, "Let's try that again."

All the pieces of paper were returned to the hat, and Julia shook the hat to shuffle the paper about.

"Then we turn the lights off," continued Rumer. "The players have to stay out of the way of the murderer who needs to find a victim. The murderer needs to tap another player three times so that the player knows they've been murdered." She walked over to the heavy drapes and pulled them across the window so that they met in the middle. It was already quite dark outside.

"Can we go downstairs?" asked Bryn.

"No," said Rumer in her best bossy voice. "We need to keep it up here. In this room. And we can't make too much noise. We don't want the oldies to know what we're up to. The victim has to say 'dead' when they're killed, then the lights go on and we have to guess who the murderer is. Okay, this time no telling," she said to Bryn.

Bryn jostled against Isabella as he tried to beat Angus to the hat. I was happy when I pulled out my note and read "player". Then someone turned the light out, and that's when I remembered that I was afraid of the dark.

At home, I can always pull my curtains back and see the streetlight and the lights of houses around me. So it's never really too dark. And there's a darkness you face when you turn out the lights that will gradually allow the ghostly outlines of shapes to appear before you. Like when you're outside in the dead of night with no moon to light the way. Then there's a darkness that's an absence of light. Am I making sense? It's like being in the bottom of a well or a deep cave or a mine. I don't know about the well or cave, but I did a mine tour once, and they turned out the lights – that's the darkness I'm talking about here. But the darkness in the Blue Room was something different again. There was an oily movement to it as if something could form out of the nothingness. A heaviness to it that felt solid. This was the darkness I faced that night. So I closed my eyes to a more comforting dark.

When I heard a giggle nearby, I dropped to the floor and headed towards the dressing table. At least, that's where I thought I was going. A shoe made contact with my leg, and I froze until it moved off again. There was a moan behind me, like a tortured ghost, and I felt the hair on the back of my neck rise in fright. There was more laughter and someone, it sounded like Julia, said, "Shut up, Lee."

I began my scuttle again until I bumped into some furniture, which I soon discovered was not the dressing table but the large armchair up against the window wall. I pushed the chair away from the wall a little, then burrowed under it like a rabbit.

There were rustlings and muffled footfalls as people moved around the room. Across from me there was a knock against wood followed by a curse, and I imagined someone had run into the wardrobe.

I could hear heavy breathing, so I held my breath in case I was listening to myself. But the heavy breathing continued, and I curled my body into a tight ball. My logical self knew that it was just one of the players, but Bryn's words echoed in my mind. "Did you say this room was haunted?"

Was the breathing thing coming to get me?

Was it a monster?

A ghost?

I opened my eyes to the oily darkness, and it pressed down on me. I was still holding my breath and felt like I might explode, but I'd forgotten how to breathe. I stretched out and tried to scrabble my way out from under the chair, shutting my eyes to see flashes of colour like neon worms, but a solid something blocked my way.

Then there was a thud and the creak of bedsprings and a muffled, "Ooof". I heard Angus say, "Dead on the bed." And someone laughed. With the flick of the light switch I gasped and gulped the fusty air, realising that the solid barrier blocking me in was in fact a heavy tallboy.

I heard someone say, "Who cracked the mirror?" As I peered out from under the chair I noticed the floor-length mirror had a crack in the bottom right-hand corner. Someone was going to be in big trouble from Grandma. I scrambled out from under the chair and as I grabbed at a drape to pull myself up I revealed the hiding space of two more players. It was Bryn and Rumer and they were locked in a kiss, or rather, Rumer seemed to be locked onto Bryn like a limpet on a jetty pylon, for Bryn's arms stayed loosely at his sides. Bryn pushed Rumer off, his red face a picture of confusion, and Rumer stepped back and gave a little laugh. She had a triumphant smirk which I didn't understand until I glanced at my sister and saw the tight disappointment on her face.

"So, who's dead?" asked Rumer.

Chapter 5

Things between Isabella and Rumer were never the same after that game. Bryn had been Isabella's first real crush, and even though he tried being extra nice to Isabella whenever they met, and though she was polite to him, I could tell that she hated him even more than she hated Rumer. He stopped coming to Vinegar House, and Isabella never mentioned him at home. I tried to tell her, in my eight-year-old way, that it wasn't Bryn's fault and that Rumer had latched on to him, but she would just say, "He's older. He should know better."

If Bryn had been Isabella's first crush, then Luke Hart was mine.

There, I've said it.

Maybe you guessed already?

The idea of it had hit me a couple of summers after that first game of Murder in the Dark. I remember it like one of those home-shot movies from the olden days – you know the ones – where the handheld camera is just a little wonky and the sound just a little fuzzy. I was strolling along the wet sand of Ocean Side at the end of a sizzling summer day. The breeze was blowing the fringe back off my face, and I swear I heard some of that smoochy music that they play in romantic movies, which could have been in my head, or could have been from the caravan park hidden behind the sand dunes. I vowed my eternal love to Luke Hart then and there. I was going to marry him. That was my silent promise to the sun and the sea spray and the tiny sand critters that made the beach come alive at that time of day. In my defence, I was barely a teenager at the time, and I didn't know a lot about life. Now I don't think I'm even going to get married – ever. Well, certainly not before I'm thirty.

I didn't need to dream about my true love, with his tanned skin, strong broad shoulders and sun-bleached hair that was lighter on the ends. I didn't need to imagine the wistful sound of his laughter, for it carried on the air towards me, a mere three rock pools away.

As he held onto the hand of my cousin, Rumer.

Which was perfectly understandable.

I know I've already told you about Rumer, but they were just the bad bits.

When the Kramer family is together they are one big lump. They have the same look about them: square bodies, straight, definite noses, and smiles that turn their lips up at the corners. There is nothing out of control. Even their hair is tidy. And then there is Rumer. Rumer is the beautiful angel that tops our family tree. She is all golden beauty and dimples. That is the good thing about Rumer. She is beautiful.

Back to the bad things. She has a temper. Her father, Uncle Lawrence, is nice enough, but he's kind of vague. When the rest of us are getting into trouble, he just looks awkward and asks her to behave. Rumer's always gotten away with things and she always takes what she wants. And that's where Luke Hart came in.

Luke Hart was mine. He had lived across the road from our house for as long as I could remember. He was older than me, just by two years, and I only ever remember him being nice to me.

Let me tell you about Luke Hart.

Luke Hart had buckteeth when he was younger. I admired him so much that I took to resting my own two top front teeth on my bottom lip, which made talking quite tricky and eating even harder. I have a very nice Year One school photo of me, sitting in the front row, third from the left, with my two teeth jutting out over my bottom lip. Mum said it made me look like a rabbit and didn't want to pay for the photo, but I cried until she let me buy a copy. I stopped the bucktoothed look on my seventh birthday when Uncle Lawrence clapped me so hard on the back that my teeth cut through my bottom lip.

I may have given up on having buckteeth, but I didn't give up on Luke Hart. He was my hero. If Luke was forced to play Monopoly with me, I let him choose the racing car token, even though that was my favourite piece. If there was a last slice of cake on the plate, it was his. If Luke needed something, I would get it for him. That didn't include Rumer though. He managed to get her all by himself.

Strike that.

She managed to get him.

I'll tell you how that happened, but first I need to tell you about Rumer's special circumstances.

The first time I'd heard the words "special circumstances" I'd already played at least ten games of Murder in the Dark, though it still wasn't my favourite game. I was just finishing up my second helping of Christmas pudding when the adults' voices dropped and I saw Uncle Lawrence bow his head as my grandmother talked about Rumer's special circumstances. Then her eyes narrowed and she asked if I hadn't had quite enough food for one day, so I slid from my chair and left the room.

While I'm quite good at eavesdropping, the closed doors at Grandma Vinegar's house are solid and word-tight. Five minutes after I had left the room, Isabella found me crouched down at the dining room door trying to listen to the adults' conversation. I hushed her as I pressed my ear closer.

There was a rush of steps behind me and then my brother Oscar asked, "What are you doing?" He probably thought I was part of his Spies game.

"Go away," said Isabella, kindly.

"What's she doing?" he repeated.

"None of your business," I said, crossly.

"If you don't tell me, I'm going to tell Mum," he said. As little brothers go, Oscar was typical. Isabella promises that he'll turn into a person one day, but I severely doubt it.

"I'll give you a dollar if you go away," I said. "I'll give it to you when we get home."

"Okay," he said. I heard the squeak of his shoes moving away towards the kitchen.

"Come on, Freya," said Isabella. "We're playing Cluedo in the Blue Room."

"*Sshhh.*"

I listened to the voices rumbling behind the door, then I heard Isabella say, "Oh," and a scratchy voice behind me say, "May I ask what you are doing?"

There were many doors in Vinegar House, at least two to a room downstairs, and Grandma had a way of sneaking about the place like a cat burglar on the prowl. One moment she'd be reading quietly in the drawing room, and the next she'd be dispositing your mobile phone, which you'd totally forgotten was in your pocket, onto the silver tray in the entry hall. Aunty Wendy, cousin Julia's mum, told me that it was a well-known fact that Grandma Vinegar had the third eye; she "saw" things that hadn't happened yet and knew things that she couldn't possibly know. I don't know if Aunty Wendy was joking, but it seemed possible to me.

"Freya?" said Grandma.

I mumbled something about losing a necklace, then Isabella and I scurried off to the Blue Room out of grandma's sight.

"She's a witch," I said hotly, my heart still beating double time at being caught eavesdropping. "What are special circumstances?" I asked Isabella before we entered the bedroom.

"What are you talking about?"

"Grandma was talking about Rumer's special circumstances. What special circumstances?" I demanded.

Isabella just shook her head as she pushed me into the bedroom. "Come on," she said, but I was sure she knew exactly what I was talking about.

Chapter 6

This is how Rumer ruined Luke Hart for me.

Somehow she had crashed *my* family's annual beach holiday with the Hart family at Ocean Side. There was hardly enough room in the holiday shack for our family, but Rumer managed to get prime position in the kids' room, just under the one tiny window that could catch a passing breeze on the stillest night. We usually put Oscar under the window because Deefa slept on Oscar's bed, and the dog usually drank a bathtub of salt water during the day. Salt water had an awful effect on Deefa's innards. I can't even begin to describe the smell.

It wasn't what I would call a "happy families" holiday. Isabella ignored Rumer most of the time – my sister could hold a grudge – although she would be polite if Rumer asked her a question. On the second day of politeness, I asked my sister how she could bear to even be in the same room as Rumer, but Isabella muttered something about Rumer's special circumstances and wouldn't explain even when I niggled her for a whole hour about it. Still, the phrase stuck in my mind …

Being the middle child in our family is like being a second-rate person. Oscar and Dad sometimes go off and do boys' things on weekends, and Oscar also has everyone's attention for he is the baby of the family. As the oldest child, Isabella knows things about our family that Oscar and I don't. I often find Isabella and Mum huddled in secret corners talking in whispers and then stopping when I appear. Just once, I would like there to be something special about being the kid stuck in the middle.

Isabella would never tell me about Rumer's secret. So one day, the second day of that fateful beach holiday at Ocean Side, I just up and asked my cousin. I waited until the others were walking down to the beach, their laughter wafting through the small open window, then I rummaged around under my camp bed while Rumer ignored me.

"Rumer," I finally asked her, pulling out some sandals, "what are your special circumstances?"

Rumer had never made a point of being my friend, so I was used to her ignoring me unless she wanted something. When I asked her again, she lowered the magazine she was reading and looked at me as if I were a mosquito she might squash.

"What are you talking about, you crazy child?" she asked.

Then she yawned.

She did it in such an insulting way, that I began to feel my familiar anger with her fizz like lemonade bubbles in my blood.

So I took a guess and asked about her mother – a thing my own mother had forbidden me to ask my cousin – and Rumer sucked the air between her teeth as if I'd stung her. Then she looked at me, her head tilted a little, and her eyes grew misty as she settled the magazine to one side and patted the camp bed in invitation. This surprised me so much that I perched on the edge of the bed without thinking.

"The truth is," said Rumer finally, "my mother is in heaven."

It was my turn to gasp.

"Oh, Rumer," I said. "How awful."

I'm going to tell you something I've never told anyone before. I sometimes imagine the loss of my own parents – in a plane crash or an earthquake, I never spend a lot of time thinking how this happens – and I immediately feel such an ache in my heart that

I have to remind myself that my parents are, in fact, alive. Even the Colonel looks good after his temporary demise. (Demise is a word I like to use instead of the word death. I don't like the phrase passed away – which is what journalists sometimes say on the news – because it sounds like someone has just gone past you, but they might be back at any moment. Anyway, that's what I think.)

"I don't remember her," I said, thinking back to the many Kramer family gatherings and special occasions.

Well, of course, there was our family – Dad, Mum, Isabella, Oscar and me.

And I've told you about Uncle Stephen, the doctor. He's married to Aunty Jenny and they have the twins, Lee and Angus.

Aunty Wendy is married to Uncle John and they have four kids – Julia and her three brothers.

Rumer and Uncle Lawrence were the relatives who always turned up late. Rumer dressed like she was going to a wedding while the rest of us were dressed like it was the first day of school holidays. Rumer and Uncle Lawrence. But never an Aunty so-and-so. It had never occurred to me that someone was missing. Not that I could remember anyway.

"I was very young," said Rumer. "Very."

"Was she beautiful? Your mother?" I asked. It made sense to me — why Rumer looked so different from the rest of us. She must have had a beautiful blond mother, a mysterious person who I would never meet.

"Of course."

"You must take after her," I said.

"I do," said Rumer, tossing her hair.

"You must miss her," I said.

Rumer shrugged. "I don't really remember her too much."

I wanted to ask Rumer about her mother's *demise*, but I wasn't sure how I could ask that, and she didn't offer any explanation. Instead, I said, "I'm glad you've come to Ocean Side with us." It was a lie, but the only nice thing I could think to say.

"I didn't realise we'd be staying in a shack," she said, with another flick of her hair.

I looked around the room. It's true, it wasn't a glamorous place, but I loved the beach house, with its sloping walls and its sandy floors. Okay, so the shelves were a little wonky and there was a gap at the bottom of the windowpane where the wind blew the sand through, but it was our shack. A fun place to be. A no-schoolwork zone, where you could eat takeaway food more than once a week. Even the Colonel stopped striding about when he was here.

"Dad and I were supposed to fly to the islands for the holidays, but he was busy." Rumer picked up the magazine and started flicking through it again.

I wondered which islands she meant, but she seemed to think I should know what she was talking about, so I didn't ask.

"You should come down to the beach," I said. "The sand's really soft. And the tide goes out so far sometimes you could walk to Barwon Village if you wanted."

Rumer yawned. "I saw it yesterday."

"And sometimes the waves leave behind coloured glass that's been rolled around and around so that it's all creamy looking and smooth around the edges. I could show you my collection, if you like."

Rumer made a noise in the back of her throat that could have been a "yes" or just a clearing of phlegm.

"And the Harts will be here soon with their caravan."

"That's nice." More page flicking.

"You know the Harts?" I prompted.

Rumer yawned again.

"Megan and Luke and little Ebony."

Rumer stopped yawning and sat up a little.

"The Harts?" she repeated.

"You know. Our neighbours from across the road at home."

I watched Rumer's nostrils flare a little, and then a small smile flit about her lips – a butterfly that was here, then gone.

"That boy," she said. "The one with the light-coloured hair."

I nodded.

"The one that helped you hit the piñata at your last birthday?"

I nodded again.

The pages flicked faster, and again the smile hovered.

"When did you say they were coming?" she asked, finally.

"Today," I said. "With their caravan. They stay surfside of the beach. Luke and his sister Megan are mad about surfing."

"I can surf," said Rumer, pausing to check an ad for lip gloss.

"Really?" I don't have what you might call a poker face, and I guess I don't have a poker voice either, because Rumer looked up from her magazine.

"You remember. Dad and I went to Hawaii last year. I took some lessons," she said, firmly. Then she wriggled her legs against my back so that I tipped off the bed and fell to the floor with a thud.

"Sorry," she said. "My foot went to sleep."

I stood up awkwardly and dusted the sand off my shorts.

"Were you going to the beach?" she asked pointedly.

I had been dismissed.

✴ ✴ ✴

The Harts arrived in a flurry of car honks after lunch, with their surfboards perched on top of their over-packed station wagon and their slightly worn caravan in tow. Everyone rushed outside to see them, and Luke emerged from the back seat, blinking at the bright sun as if he'd just woken, a crushed drink can in one hand.

"Hi, Shrimp," he muttered, ruffling my hair.

Ebony tumbled out behind him, water wings already attached to her arms and zinc on her nose. "I'm going swimming," she announced. "Luke has braces." Then she pointed behind me. "Who's that?"

I turned around to Rumer dressed in black from head to … well … the top of her thigh. Her tight black T-shirt looked like it had been sprayed on, and her cut-off jeans nipped in at the waist to show off the rest of her great figure. Her hair was shoved up in a loose bun,

57

but strands of it curled about her face and the nape of her neck. I wondered how long it had taken her to look so casual. A striped beach towel was draped over one shoulder and a pair of dark sunglasses hid half of her face.

"You remember Rumer," I said to Ebony. "You met her at my birthday."

Ebony shook her head. Megan and Isabella had already found each other and had gone inside the shack for a cold drink. Luke was standing near the car looking like he'd been run over by a train, which wasn't a look I'd ever seen on him before.

"You know Rumer, Luke?" I asked. "You met her—"

"Hi," he said, interrupting me. He gave her a huge smile, and I could see his beautiful teeth strapped in with wires and coloured bands. It made him look like a stranger.

Rumer let her sunglasses slide down her nose and she peered at him with her bright blue eyes.

"Oh. Hello," she said, as if I hadn't mentioned that she'd be meeting Luke again. "Well, I'm off to the beach. Going to check out the surf. See what kind of waves are happening."

"The surf's not that way," I said, but she ignored me.

Ebony followed the adults inside, while Luke and I watched Rumer walking down the track to the beach. I was impatient to show Luke my latest sea glass finds, but he continued to look at the beach path long after Rumer had disappeared behind the dunes.

I tugged at Luke's sleeve. "Do you want–"

"Wait," Luke called out to the emptiness that Rumer had left.

Then he shoved his empty drink can at me and ran after her.

Luke continued to run after Rumer for the rest of the three weeks we were at Ocean Side. Instead of Luke and me hanging out, it was Luke, Rumer and me. Which meant it was Luke and Rumer, while I tagged along feeling like a third wheel. And that's when I decided I loved Luke Hart and was going to marry him. Being left out just made me more determined. That scene at the rock pools. The whole smoochy music and windblown hair thing? You remember.

I wanted to tell Rumer that Luke was mine, but the thing was he didn't know it. Luke had turned into a complete stranger, as if Rumer had drugged him or something. He followed her around, fetching her drinks, buying her ice-creams, rubbing her back with sunblock – it was just plain embarrassing. Even I knew what was going on. Rumer was bored. Luke was there. She was just going to have some fun before she went back to her real home with Uncle Lawrence and her circumstances.

I tried to talk to Isabella about it, but she told me it was none of my business. So then I decided to try and warn Luke myself. He was such a nice person. I couldn't believe that I had somehow brought Luke and Rumer together. But Luke and Rumer were always together, which made telling him tricky. And then when I did get a spare moment with him, I didn't know what to say.

"Luke, you look like an idiot running after Rumer" was too harsh.

"Luke, Rumer's a cow." Also harsh.

One day, as we buried Ebony armpit-deep in sand, Rumer strolled down to the water to wash her hands in the waves, and Luke and I were alone. Alone with Ebony, of course, but she didn't count.

"Luke, I need to tell you something," I said, carefully patting another bucketload of sand into the shape of an aeroplane wing.

"Uh-huh." He was concentrating on getting the aeroplane body just right as it fanned out behind Ebony's body.

"Luke, Rumer isn't what you think she is," I said.

I was watching Rumer as she skipped over the waves then bent down to rinse her hands.

"What are you saying?" He looked up and waved at Rumer who waved back.

"She has … special circumstances," I blurted out. I couldn't believe I had told him. It wasn't my secret to tell, and now Rumer would make me pay in a way I didn't even want to consider.

"What?" he said, looking at me.

"Her mother is dead," I said.

"Wow." Luke clapped the loose sand from his hands and shook his head. "She never mentioned that."

"I just thought you should know," I said lamely. "You really like Rumer, don't you?"

Luke ducked his head and tweaked Ebony's nose.

That's when I knew that it was useless. If Luke asked me to help him win Rumer's undying love, I would have done anything to help him. As it was, he didn't need my help.

"Thanks, Shrimp," he said. He patted me on the shoulder then he stood up and jogged over to Rumer, who was trying to dodge the waves as they broke on the shore.

I watched Luke lean towards Rumer, their heads close together. I saw her sharply look my way then hang her head. She looked back at him and yelled, her arms moving about like a squid out of water. He stepped back, surprised, but kept talking to her. I watched her bend forwards and slap him hard across the face. He walked back to me and put his hand on my shoulder.

"Sorry, Freya," he said. "I've just realised how incredibly beautiful you are. Much more beautiful than Rumer will ever be …"

Actually, this didn't happen.

I watched Luke lean towards Rumer, their heads close together. I saw her sharply look my way then hang her head.

Luke's arm looped over her shoulders in a hug. And then they kissed. Which is when I decided I would never love anyone again, because you just felt like an idiot when you put love out there and it didn't come back your way.

"I want to get out," demanded Ebony from her sand trap. "I'm sick of this game."

"So am I, Ebs," I said.

And I grabbed the spade.

❋ ❋ ❋

Life changed after that, and I blame Rumer. But

maybe it was always going to change; maybe she'd just hurried things along. Rumer dumped Luke at the end of those summer holidays, like I knew she would. There was an uncomfortable weekend in autumn of that same year when Mum decided to invite Luke to Vinegar House – the same weekend that Rumer happened to be there – but then things settled down.

I stopped dropping in on the Hart family across the road. I made sure I was busy in my room when they came over for card nights. I made other plans when the Harts came to dinner. If Luke saw me in the street, he'd wave, but I'd look the other way until he got the message. I stopped going down to the jetty at high tide on Saturday mornings. I dodged him at school.

So I got over my first crush eventually, and I guess I had Rumer to thank for that. I guess she did me a favour.

And that's all I'm going to say about Luke Hart.

Chapter 7

There was a lot to organise before my parents could just fly away and leave me to the dullness of Vinegar House. Luckily, the Colonel was onto it. Dad had rung the holiday camp to let the coordinators know what was going on. Oscar was to go to his friend's house if Mum and Dad weren't back in time to pick him up. Then Dad left a couple of messages with Isabella on her mobile, because it was still too early for her to be awake. Dad was striding around, busy being the person in charge, so I was trying to stay out of his way. If I came across Mum, I'd give her a hug and she'd pat me on the back as if I were the one with the sick mother.

At around lunchtime the doorbell rang and I answered it to find Mrs Hart and Luke standing at the door. (I know I wasn't going to talk about him any more, but he just happens to be in this part of the story.)

"Can we come in?" Mrs Hart asked brightly before giving me a hug that went on for ten seconds too long.

Awkward.

Luke looked taller than I remembered and there was something different about him, but I couldn't pinpoint what it was. He seemed uncomfortable to be there.

"Mum," I called out.

"Ericaaaa," sang Mrs Hart.

Mrs Hart is a member of the Homsea Acapella Group and the Port Eden Players – a theatre group. She is very DRAMATIC.

Mrs Hart sailed past me, gathered Mum into her arms and gave her a long hug. Mum burst into tears, and Luke and I sidled out to the kitchen to leave them to it.

"Do you want a drink?" I asked him.

Luke shrugged. "I'm sorry to hear about your grandma, Shrimp."

"My Nanna," I corrected. Shrimp. I hated that nickname and wished he'd never started calling me that. "That's okay. Thanks."

"So what's going to happen?" he asked. "Mum said your parents are leaving tomorrow morning."

"Yep."

I filled the kettle with water for something to do.

"How long's the flight?" he asked.

"I'm not sure." I fussed around, pulling out cups and teaspoons.

"How's Isabella?"

"Yeah, good."

"Have you been busy? Haven't seen you since … I don't know, for ages."

"Yeah. Busy. Really busy."

I put instant coffee in the teapot, realised what I'd done, then filled it up with hot water anyway and hoped Luke wouldn't ask for a cup. I didn't need this now. I didn't need Luke Hart with his messy hair and his smooth brown skin and his bobbing Adam's apple filling up the space in my kitchen.

"How's Oscar?" he asked.

"Yeah, good." It was ridiculous. I searched my brain for something smart to say. Something mind-blowing that would make him think about me long after he'd finished filling up my kitchen. Not that I cared about him the way I used to. Still, I didn't want him to think I was still that little kid that used to follow him around.

"Are you busy?" I asked.

"Yeah," he said nodding. "Really busy."

"Oh." I grabbed the milk carton out of the fridge,

then stood looking in a cupboard for a milk jug until I forgot what I was looking for. "How's Megan?"

"Good."

"And Ebony?"

"Yeah, good. Great."

"Great." I tried to imagine us on the debating team together at school. No trophies there.

"I'm looking for a job. School holidays," he said. "Loz Pinkerton's brother wants to sell his car. Says he'll give me first say."

"Do you have your Ls?" I asked.

"Yup."

"Oh." I wondered when that had happened. "What sort of job?"

Luke shrugged. "I could garden. Mow lawns or something. Wash cars …"

"Dumfy's got the lawn service thing all stitched up," I said. Dumfy was Porky Sudholz's brother-in-law. "Maybe you could work for Porky – at the butcher's?"

"Working with dead things?" Luke shook his head. "I don't think so."

There was silence as we both contemplated my sick Nanna who could be dead even as we spoke.

"I wished you'd called me earlier," said Mrs Hart as she and Mum bustled into the kitchen.

Mum gave Luke a hug. He had to bend down to hug her back.

"I was just saying to your mother, Freya, that you could have stayed with us," Mrs Hart rattled on. "Although there's not a lot of room at present, not with my sister and her family staying."

Luke snorted and brushed past me on his way to the tap. Making himself at home, I thought, but of course this *had* been his second home for years. I wondered if the snort was the thought of me staying or the fact that his aunt and family had taken over his home.

"Is that a fresh pot?" Mum asked.

"Umm, no. I'll make one," I said, turning away from Luke's surprised expression. I emptied the coffee, rinsed the teapot, and put the kettle on again.

"Anyway, I think it's lovely you've got the chance to stay with your cousin at your grandma's house," said Mrs Hart.

"Hmm." I hoped Luke wasn't listening.

"Which one is it again? Julia?"

"Rumer," corrected Mum. "They're very close."

I wondered if she meant Julia and Rumer were very close. I felt Luke watching me.

"Oh, that's right. Wasn't she the one who came to Ocean Side with you? You remember Rumer, don't you Luke?" Mrs Hart asked pointedly.

Luke scowled.

"She was such a pretty girl. Nothing like her cousins at all," she said.

Luke snorted.

"Not that you're not pretty, Freya," Mrs Hart continued quickly, looking at me. "You have such nice … eyelashes."

Luke snorted again.

"Two summers ago," said Mum, absently.

"Was it that long ago?" Mrs Hart sighed. "We must have you over for dinner when you come back, Erica. Life just has a way of getting away from you."

"Don't I know it," Mum agreed. Then the tears began to leak down her cheeks again, and Mrs Hart pressed some tissues into her hand.

I filled the tea orders, then said, "I need to pack."

To be perfectly honest, I'd been packed for hours, but I just needed a quiet space with no crying or penetrating stares.

"Wait, how are you getting to Florence's house?" Mrs Hart asked.

It took me a moment to realise she was talking about my grandmother.

"Dad?" I said. We hadn't really talked about it.

"Nonsense," said Mrs Hart. "Your father doesn't have time for that. I'll drive you."

"No, it's too far," said Mum in a voice that meant yes.

"I insist," said Mrs Hart. "It's such a lovely drive. There's a darling little antique shop on the way. I wonder if it's open today? Anyway, Erica, it's one less thing you have to do. Really. It's fine. And of course we'll feed the dog for you."

I left them to their plans and didn't bother looking up when Luke said goodbye.

In the study I took a chance and logged on to Facebook. There were a few people online. People were taking sides about what had happened at the party the week before. Everyone thought they knew the real story and didn't bother to ask me. Somebody called me a name I don't want to repeat here. I wanted to die. I wanted to melt down into my computer chair until I was just a puddle of shame.

As I turned off the computer, I realised I'd be without the internet while I was at Vinegar House. And I was glad.

Chapter 8

Mrs Hart picked me up at two that afternoon. Mum promised to ring Grandma and explain that I would need to keep my mobile with me so that I could contact them overseas. She was counting on the fact that Grandma wouldn't want to pay for international calls. So was I. Mum seemed to forget that I needed some kind of computer to work on if I was to get my homework done, but Dad was taking the laptop, and I couldn't see myself lugging the home computer to Vinegar House. I was going to have to hand write my homework. Still, if I didn't get all my homework done by next term, I'd have a good excuse.

When Mrs Hart bip-bipped her car horn, I dragged my luggage out to the car to find Luke was coming along for the ride.

"Help Freya," said Mrs Hart, crossly, and Luke unfolded himself from the front passenger seat. He grabbed my bags and threw them into the boot as if they were filled with marshmallows instead of half my wardrobe.

I think he was just showing off.

I didn't understand why Luke was coming along. I'm sure the idea of more than an hour's drive one-way, with the possibility of antique shopping would make anyone stay home. Obviously his mother had made him come along. I wondered how she'd bribed him.

I hugged my parents one last time, and Dad slipped me some money, though I didn't know where I'd spend it.

"Just in case you go to town," he said, lamely.

I was so busy settling into the back seat that I barely noticed their "take care" and "help your grandmother". By the time I popped an earbud into one ear, Mrs Hart was taking off at her usual breakneck speed, and I was scrabbling to get my seatbelt on. As I clicked it into place, I looked through the car's rear window for a final wave, and it felt like someone had invaded my chest and squeezed all the juice out of my heart until it was a tiny dry sponge. My parents looked so sad standing together – my mother leaning into my father's side – that I couldn't bear to watch them waving me goodbye.

✳ ✳ ✳

I spent the next twenty minutes trying not to look at Luke's profile in the front seat, while Mrs Hart prattled on like an infomercial on late-night TV. In the end I pretended to sleep and Luke turned on some music. Then I really did fall asleep until I realised we'd stopped, and there was sleep dribble on my shoulder. We were parked outside a shop declaring it had *Antiques and Collectables*, but Luke was still sitting in the front passenger seat and he was smirking at me.

"What?" I wanted to smooth my hair, which felt messed up, but wouldn't do it while he was watching me. I didn't want him to think I cared about how I looked to him.

"You snore, Shrimp," he said.

"I do not," I said, crossly. There was a bad taste in my mouth like I had swallowed a glue stick. "And stop calling me that."

"Ah, yes you do, Shrimp," he said, ignoring my request.

I used to like Luke Hart. Idolised him. Felt a warm glow whenever he was around. But this Luke Hart annoyed me, and I was glad we weren't friends any more.

"I have a cold," I said, improvising. Then I sniffed a couple of times to make a point. "And you … you have a zit on your nose. I'm surprised you can see past it, it's so big."

It was the meanest thing I could think of to say, but it didn't remove the smirk from his face, and I felt a strong urge to lean forwards and push my hand into that smirk until it went away.

Luckily for Luke, his mobile buzzed and he turned around in his seat to send someone a message. I checked my own phone to see that we were only forty-five minutes into our trip. I texted Isabella and Holly, but there were no quick replies. I needed a drink, then cursed when I realised I'd left my water bottle in the fridge at home.

✳ ✳ ✳

I spent the rest of the trip squashed up against a bathroom pitcher and basin that Mrs Hart just couldn't live without. I thought it was hideous, but she seemed very happy with it. When she asked what I thought about it, I smiled and said it was an amazing colour. And this was true. I was amazed anyone could like the salmon-pink colour with baby blue highlights picked out on tiny rosebuds and swirling ribbons. I knew Luke was onto me, so I resisted looking at him and stared out the window instead. Eventually, the car turned down the familiar gravel road, and we crunched along for another five minutes. As we crested the last hill, the grey shingle roof of Vinegar House suddenly appeared. This was always my favourite part of the trip to the house, because one moment you're surrounded by dry hilly country and the next the sea is laid out before you like a shimmering secret. I cranked down the window a little to sniff at the salty air.

I must admit that the house always looked imposing at a distance. It seemed rooted into the very earth it stood upon, its many tiny windows flanked by shutters and its stone bricks made it look like it was carved straight out of the hill. It was only as you drew closer that you saw the cracks. Mortar crumbled between the bricks in the chimneys, some of the window casements were warped from the weather and the roof looked like it wouldn't last a minor rain shower. Even the trees around the house looked grey and worn that day, their bare branches rattling in spindly defiance against the sea breeze.

"Here we are," said Mrs Hart, who was good at stating the obvious.

It wasn't until Rumer strolled out to the car as we pulled up that I realised, like I'd been hit with an antique bathroom pitcher, exactly why Luke Hart had come along for the ride.

"Well, look who's here," said Mrs Hart, her eyes wide with surprise, as if she hadn't expected to see Rumer. "Here we are," she sang out again. Then she bounded from the car to grab Rumer in a huge hug.

"Well, look who's here," I muttered loud enough for Luke to hear.

I watched his face turn from red to white and back again.

"Come on, you twoooo," sang Mrs Hart. (I would not pay to hear Mrs Hart sing. If you tell anyone I said that, I'll deny it.)

I climbed out from under the antique treasure, and Rumer removed herself from her torturer to come and give me a fake hug – the kind where you hang onto a person's arms, lean in, but don't make any other contact.

"Hi, cuz," she said brightly. Then in my ear, "There is nothing to do here. Old vinegar-tongue is driving me nuts."

I saw Luke hovering behind Rumer, so I said, "Great to see you too. Luke was just saying, he couldn't wait to catch up."

Rumer swirled around and Luke gave her a sheepish

grin. Then she grabbed him in a non-fake hug that meant her body was pushed so close up against his that you couldn't get a toothpick between them if you tried. It was probably illegal in over forty-seven countries. She leaned back and looked him full in the face.

"Smile again!" she ordered.

He smiled and I realised that his braces had been removed. In their place was a perfect set of white non-bucked teeth. Maybe that was the difference I'd noticed earlier that day. My childhood hero was gone.

"Well done, you. Grandma said you must come in and say hello. Mrs Skelton cooked a lemon tart this morning. Let's hope it's better than her muffin recipe." She tucked her arm through Luke's and escorted both the Harts to the front door, talking all the while, as I struggled behind with the luggage.

I had a strong feeling of deja vu.

Chapter 9

I shoved my mobile phone further down in my pocket as I stood in the entry hall – just in case Grandma decided I couldn't keep it with me. I could hear Mrs Hart's and Rumer's voices competing against the low murmurs of my grandmother from the drawing room. As I dropped my largest suitcase to the floor, Mrs Skelton appeared at the top of the stairs, a duster in one hand, and a frown on her face.

"Hello, Mrs Skelton," I said, loudly.

The poor woman was older than my grandmother – probably should have retired years ago. She'd come to Vinegar House ten years before, when Grandma had tripped on the front step and broken her wrist. The family had insisted that Grandma move closer to town.

"This is my home," Grandma had said gruffly. "The only way I'm leaving here is in a pine box."

Of course, that idea was ridiculous, a total lie, because Grandma would never settle for anything less than something in mahogany, with shiny brass handles and maroon satin lining. Still, she got her own way. Even the Colonel couldn't make Grandma do something she didn't want to.

The compromise was Mrs Skelton, who was supposed to be a live-in companion, but who also cooked most of the meals and kept a tidy house. This suited Grandma Vinegar who always walked about as if she were the Queen of England. Much better than just having a house cleaner come in once a week. She probably bragged about it to her friends.

Mrs Skelton was a tall woman with silver hair which she wore pulled back severely across her head. Her face was the colour of the calico at Miss Maudy's Quilt Barn and was highlighted by cheekbones that reminded me of the Jolly Roger's flag (which features a skull, if you don't know). I'd caught her napping more than once in the afternoon sun in the drawing room or the library. Grandma had found Isabella and I giggling one day as Mrs Skelton sat in one of the library's huge leather chairs, her head tipped back, and a snore rising from her like a motor.

"Mrs Skelton deserves a rest, don't you think, girls?" Grandma had asked, her tone low and icy. "Perhaps you could help lessen her load?"

My sister and I spent the rest of the day cleaning the silverware until our hands were black from it and fingers sore from the rubbing.

"Hello, Mrs Skelton," I repeated even louder.

She gave me a little wave, peering down through the gloom.

"Is that you, Erica?" she said.

"It's Freya," I told her, horrified that she would think I was my mother.

"Oh, yes."

She told me to take my things to the Yellow Room, grumbling loudly as she polished at an errant mark on the staircase handrail.

"I don't get paid enough for all this upset," she said as I slid past her into my room.

Knowing my grandmother, she was probably right.

I dumped my things inside the bedroom door, then my phone buzzed – a missed phone call from Mum that had gone straight to message bank. I moved around the room for a better signal then returned Mum's call, assuring her that I'd arrived safely and telling her to have a safe trip. It was on the tip of my tongue to ask her to take me with them. Luckily, the phone call dropped out before I could.

I pulled the curtains back to let in the grey wintry

light. The nap of the velvet had worn in places from countless fingers doing the exact same thing. I wondered whose room it had been before Dad's. Maybe I'd keep that question up my sleeve for when I was sitting in the drawing room with Grandma and Rumer and had nothing to say.

The weak light at the window couldn't chase away the gloom, so I turned on a bedside lamp then pushed at the springs of the bed that sagged in the middle. The room was cold. I got up and ran my hand over the heating coil against the wall. It was barely tepid. Just warm enough, really, to keep the damp from the walls. I'd have to ask Mrs Skelton for a hot water bottle for my bed. Grandma didn't believe in electric blankets.

This was the room that my family bunked in whenever we stayed at Vinegar House when I was little. There were plenty of spare bedrooms but us kids were always too scared of the house to sleep without an adult around. I found it hard to picture the young Mathew – my Dad's name – hanging out in his room with posters and a radio (if Grandma had let him).

His old study desk took up a lot of space in one corner of the room. It made a great cubbyhouse if you threw a blanket over it and climbed under into the space left for feet. It was during my cubbyhouse days that I found Dad's initials carved into the underside of the desk. I'd been learning my alphabet at school, and discovering his initials was like uncovering a lost treasure map to my father. This proved he had been a boy once. Someone short like me. Someone who didn't always stride about barking commands. But when I asked Dad about it he seemed annoyed, saying it was, "not in his nature to deface property, even as a child." He'd used the work "deface" as if I should know what it meant. I was five at the time.

For years, Dad would bring some blow-up mattresses when we stayed over, and we'd pretend we were camping. Oscar usually ended up in bed with Mum and Dad by the morning, but Isabella and I would line up our beds side by side, giggling at the dust bunnies under the high double bed, telling each other ghost stories until we were left breathless in the dark, scared by the strength of our imaginations.

We hadn't stayed over for years. Dad was always in a hurry to get back to some business thing, and Isabella used uni as an excuse to do whatever she wanted. I felt sorry for Oscar. By the time he was old enough to join in with the games of the older cousins, we'd pretty much stopped playing, although Isabella was always up for a board game if he ever got tired of doing nothing.

Isabella. I wished she were with me, putting up with Grandma and Rumer and old Mrs Skelton. Then I realised it was all her fault. If she hadn't taken a holiday, I'd be in my own home right now, checking out the pantry, or lying on the couch in front of the TV. I'd gotten through to her mobile phone before I left home, and though she was sad for Mum, she was happy to take Dad's advice and continue her holiday, agreeing with him that there was nothing she could do. At least she hadn't laughed when I told her about staying at Vinegar House.

"Oh, sorry, Freya, but it won't be that bad," she said. "I'll bring you back a present."

"Thanks," I'd said dully.

"And say hi to Rumer for me." And then she did laugh.

"I hate you," I said.

"I'll make it a big present," she said.

I lay down on the bed and smelled the strange mix of must and lavender that always reminded me of Vinegar House. The pillowcases felt damp. I noticed the paint on the ceiling was peeling in one corner of the room, and there was a stain near the window as if the roof might be leaking.

"Your grandmother says you might like to come

downstairs. Afternoon tea is ready." Mrs Skelton was at the door, the duster still in one hand.

I slid off the bed, aware that I'd had my shoes on the bedcover, and knowing that Mrs Skelton had seen me.

"Afternoon tea? Yummy," I gabbled.

I hadn't said the word yummy … well, ever really. I barely stopped myself from rubbing my stomach like some pantomime character. There was something about Mrs Skelton that always made me feel like apologising.

"I hear you've made a tart." I tried to brush at the dirt my shoes had left, pretending I was smoothing the bedcover.

"Did you now?" She eyed me suspiciously.

"Rumer told me. She said she hoped the tarts were as good as your muffins." I laughed nervously.

"Did she?" Mrs Skelton moved towards the bed and shook her head at the mess my shoes had made.

"I love a good tart," I said, edging towards the door. That just sounded rude. I stifled a nervous giggle. I didn't think Mrs Skelton would enjoy the joke. "Muffins too. Muffins and tarts. They're all good."

"Afternoon tea is a waste of time, if you ask me," said Mrs Skelton severely. "Considering your dinner is at six. Don't fill up on tart," she said. "I'm not cooking a roast for nothing."

"Oh, a roast. Great. I'm just going to …"

And with that I left the room and ran down the stairs, leaving Mrs Skelton grumbling behind me.

The Harts didn't stay for long. There was barely time for me to go downstairs and shove the rubbery lemon tart into my mouth before they were standing up and saying their goodbyes.

"See you soon," Rumer said to Luke before she disappeared upstairs.

As usual, Rumer hadn't wasted time organising her social calendar. It seemed like Luke Hart was back on the menu.

My heart skipped as Luke stopped on the steps with me then leaned in and brushed my cheek with his lips and whispered in my ear, "I will see you soon …"

Actually, that didn't really happen.

While I was dreaming of Luke Hart kissing me on the cheek he was waving goodbye, closing the car door behind him, then disappearing down the driveway in a flurry of white gravel.

Then I sat down on the house entrance steps and looked out past the bluff to the sea, which was the grey of Luke Hart's eyes. A sea breeze sent the smell of something dead from the beach or it may have just been a stale mound of seaweed. I watched the choppy waves and the seagulls wheeling above me, riding on the air currents.

And I felt the house watching me as I sat.

Chapter 10

That first night at Vinegar House, well technically, it was the next morning, I woke at 2.47 am. I know this because I checked my mobile phone, which I kept under my pillow. I wasn't sure what had woken me at first, and then I heard the *slap slap* of a loose shutter from somewhere downstairs. I was mostly awake so I decided to visit the toilet. With my torch app guiding me, I found my way to the dresser and turned on the tiny lamp there, then moved into the hallway and turned right towards the bathroom. I could hear the sound of fast-running water. It wasn't the shallow sound of water splashing into the handbasin, but the deeper sound of water pouring into the bath.

Who'd be taking a bath now? I thought.

By this time I really had to go to the toilet, and the nearest toilet was in that bathroom. The second toilet was downstairs, and I didn't like the idea of moving around the dark house with only a torch app on my phone to guide me.

I knocked softly on the bathroom door, but there was no answer. I knocked again, louder this time, then tried the handle and the door opened with a creak. The room was in darkness, so I turned on the light. Steam had fogged the cabinet mirror and condensation was already forming on the peeling wallpaper. A flimsy plastic curtain screened off the claw-foot bath up against the wall.

"Hello?" I whispered.

I know you think I'm probably crazy not to turn and run, but I was still half asleep, and my brain was on autopilot. The running water continued. I thought I heard the sound of splashing about, like someone was in the bath already.

I needed to go to the toilet but I wasn't about to go if someone was in the bath so I reached out and tugged at the curtain in a jerky move.

"What are you doing?"

I screamed.

There was no one in the bath, but when I turned around Mrs Skelton was standing by the sink watching me with a frown on her face.

"I … I heard the water …"

The housekeeper moved forwards and turned the taps off tightly.

"This house is old," she said. "The whole plumbing

system needs replacing, but …" She shrugged.

"The taps?"

"Sometimes the taps work themselves loose," said Mrs Skelton. "I'll get Mr Chilvers to look at it tomorrow."

Then she pulled at the chain attached to the bathplug so that the water could escape. We didn't discuss how the plug just happened to be in place.

She stared me down until I said, "All right."

I felt her watch me as I returned to my bedroom. I left the dresser light on and hopped back into bed, then realised I hadn't made it to the toilet after all. I'd just have to wait until morning.

And I tried not to think about the splashing noises from the bath.

Chapter 11

I don't like conflict. Some people seem to like the excitement of it. They enjoy the yelling and the drama, but it makes my insides twist, and I run and hide whenever I can until the trouble is over. I guess you could call me a coward. It's why I always gave in to my cousin Rumer and why I dread her bad temper. Waiting for Rumer to have one of her meltdowns was like waiting for a threatening thunderstorm. After a couple of days at Vinegar House I could feel the clouds rolling in from the horizon. There was a definite temperature drop and occasional glimpses of lightning when she snapped at me.

"*Please* don't use my shampoo, it's very expensive."

"*I* was going to take that piece of toast."

"Can you be *quiet*, I'm trying to study."

"Do you *have* to be so noisy when you get up in the mornings?"

"Are you *totally* stupid?"

It may not seem much to you, but I knew Rumer, and this was the start of something bigger. Something was bugging her and someone was going to pay.

She was spending a lot of time in her room and I wasn't sure what that was about.

At home I'd sleep in until lunchtime when I was on holidays. At Vinegar House I was waking up early with a cold hot water bottle – which really just made it a cold water bottle, I suppose – and a cold nose, and could only get warm if I had a hot shower. By then I was wide awake and my bed was usually made once I returned to my room. I assumed Mrs Skelton was to blame, but I never caught her at it.

Grandma insisted that Rumer and I come down to breakfast by nine every morning so that Mrs Skelton could clear the breakfast dishes. At home I hardly ever ate breakfast unless it was Sunday, and if I did, it was standing up grabbing bites of toast while doing something else. Still, it was something to do as I was already bored with my homework and we were only allowed to watch TV for a couple of hours at night.

The second morning, Rumer was late downstairs, and by the third morning she nearly missed breakfast altogether. When she did eventually get to the dining table, it wasn't to eat anything.

"Where's my red top?" she demanded.

I shrugged and nibbled at my toast crust.

Grandma carefully sectioned off the last of her poached egg and pushed it onto the back of her fork. Once she'd eaten it, she dabbed at her lips with a napkin and placed her knife and fork side by side on the plate.

"Red top?" she repeated.

"I only have one red top here," said Rumer, "and it's missing."

"Elbows," said Grandma, and Rumer lifted her elbows from the dining table with a puff of exasperation.

"Is it in the wash?" I asked timidly.

"I've gone through the clean washing and it isn't there," said Rumer.

"Dirty washing?" I asked.

She gave me a withering look, which I guessed meant it wasn't there either.

Grandma carefully sipped black tea from a floral china teacup. "Perhaps you could try your bedroom floor, Rumer? Mrs Skelton tells me that is your preferred storage option."

Rumer's eyes blazed like cold ice. "Mrs Skelton's–"

"A very good help to me. However, she does find it

hard to vacuum your floor, Rumer. Perhaps you could tidy that up after breakfast?"

Rumer pushed her chair away from the table and swept out of the room, slamming the door behind her.

Grandma Vinegar finished her tea as if nothing had happened, then said, "The wind is brisk today."

But I knew that wouldn't be the end of it.

❋ ❋ ❋

Just before noon that day I found Rumer's red top folded on my bed. I wasn't sure how it got there. I went to Rumer's bedroom, the door was ajar.

"Rumer?" I said, quietly.

I pushed at the door — a slight shudder passing through me as I looked around the Blue Room. It hadn't changed much since that first Murder in the Dark game, though the floor-length mirror had gone. The floor was tidy and only shoes remained at the foot of the bed. There was no cousin in sight, but a faint pulsing glow drew me inside. Rumer had brought her laptop with her.

"What do you want?" Rumer stood at the door behind me, slightly out of breath.

"Where have you been?" I asked.

"I went for a jog," she said.

I looked down at her high-heeled boots and couldn't imagine Rumer running anywhere.

"Is that my red top?" she snapped.

"Yes, I–"

She snatched it out of my hands and held it close to her chest.

"Mrs Skelton must have thought it was mine," I said.

Rumer grunted.

"You brought your laptop with you," I said.

She shrugged. "I need it. For study. This is a very important school year for me."

"Bet Grandma doesn't know it's here."

"Who cares?" She shrugged again, then looked quickly over her shoulder into the hall. "I need it," she repeated. "Anyway, she can't tell me what to do."

"Mrs Skelton must know you have it." I couldn't imagine Mrs Skelton not knowing everything that was going on in the house.

"And?"

"Grandma doesn't even have the internet on here."

Rumer pointed to the USB modem plugged into the computer's side. "Dad insisted I come and spend some quality time with Grandma. There was no way I was coming without my laptop."

I wondered if Rumer understood what "quality time" meant.

"I need to get changed," said Rumer. "I'm sweaty after that walk."

"I thought you went for a jog–"

"Freya!"

"Maybe I could use it sometime," I pointing to the laptop, "just now and then?"

"Hmm," she said, in a way that meant there was no way in hell I'd be able to.

"You've got to let me–" I pleaded.

Mrs Skelton stopped at the doorway.

"I need a hand moving a rug downstairs," she said looking at me. "The one in the drawing room."

Rumer moved to stand next to me, blocking the view of the laptop from Mrs Skelton's gaze.

"Will you be helping too?" Mrs Skelton asked Rumer, dryly.

"I need to get changed," said Rumer, still holding her red top.

"Right. Just you then," said Mrs Skelton addressing me. She turned away. "You might want to keep that computer thing more hidden. Your grandmother's likely to burn it if she sees it."

I followed Mrs Skelton into the hallway.

"Oh," said Mrs Skelton. "I had a message. Mrs Kramer wants a word with her." She nodded towards Rumer's room.

"I'll tell her," I said.

I went back and found Rumer frantically going through the pocket of her red top.

"Grandma wants to see you—"

"Get out!" she barked.

As I left the bedroom door slammed behind me.

✳ ✳ ✳

I didn't hear Rumer and Grandma's discussion, but when Rumer came downstairs for lunch an hour later, she seemed to have found her best manners. She asked politely for the salt, kept her elbows off the table and even smiled at one point. I watched her pick at Mrs Skelton's steak and kidney pie, which was more kidney than steak. I wondered why people thought it was okay to eat offal when there were plenty of other things to eat in the world.

I would prefer to eat cardboard rather than kidneys. Seriously.

I hid the kidneys under a piece of piecrust and doused the rest of it in tomato sauce to hide the taste.

We were eating in silence, as always, when my phone began to bark (my latest ringtone which drove Deefa nuts when he heard it), and I nearly fell off my chair. I'd been waiting on a call from Mum and had left the phone in my pocket, but I thought I'd switched it to silent mode.

"What is that noise?" said Grandma, glaring my way.

"Sorry, Grandma. I think it's Mum." I moved into the hall and checked my phone to discover that Isabella had tried to call me.

Ring u later, I texted back, then turned my phone to silent and shoved it into my pocket. I considered skipping the rest of lunch and going back up to my room, but I knew I'd have to face Grandma eventually. Back at the table, Rumer had moved her meal from one side of the plate to the other.

"Well?" asked Grandma.

"Everything's fine," I mumbled.

"Please tell your mother to feel free to ring the home line," said Grandma.

"I think it's cheaper by mobile."

Grandma nodded. Being thrifty was something she understood.

"So, Grandma, whose room am I sleeping in?" I asked.

"You know perfectly well that was your father's room." She placed her knife and fork together on the plate and pushed it to one side.

"No, I mean, whose room was it before it was Dad's?"

"It was used as a guestroom when I first arrived here as a bride. As to who used it before that…?" She waved her hand dismissively. "Is there something wrong with the room?"

"No, no. I just wondered," I said, lamely.

"Fine," said my grandmother, gathering crumbs from the tablecloth and depositing them on her plate. "And your room, Rumer?"

"Is good, thanks, Gran," said Rumer in her best demure voice, though I saw her nostrils flare.

"That's just as well – you've hardly left your room since you've arrived. Are you ill?"

"Study," said Rumer. "I have exams soon."

"Your uncle Stephen was a very studious boy," said Grandma. "Of course, he's a doctor now. Is that your plan, Rumer? To be a doctor?"

Rumer shrugged. "I'm not sure, Grandma. I thought I might do something in multimedia."

"Computers?"

"Kind of."

"I suppose that's your father's influence." Grandma shook her head as if incredibly disappointed. Uncle Lawrence worked in IT, which Grandma refused to believe was a job. "Hmm, while I admire your work ethic, I believe in moderation in all things. You should take a walk when you finish your lunch and get some fresh air. Both of you. Stay away from the bluff path though; its edges are eroding and it's quite dangerous. I should get Mr Chilvers to have a look at that. There is just so much to do around here …" She stared out through the windows without finishing her sentence.

Rumer threw her table napkin over her lunch plate to hide her uneaten food. "Great idea, Gran. I'll just go upstairs and get changed."

"Take your coats in case the weather turns, girls," said Gran. "It's quite fickle this time of year."

Rumer and I bustled out of the dining room, away from the dreaded kidney pie and Grandma Vinegar. But as I closed the door, I caught a glimpse of Grandma. She was still looking towards the window, slumped in her seat. She seemed sad.

I turned my back on her and quietly closed the door.

Chapter 12

I grabbed a coat and a scarf from my room, used the downstairs bathroom (I was avoiding the upstairs bathroom whenever possible) and waited at the front door for ten minutes before Rumer eventually made an appearance. Instead of thanking me for waiting, she swished past me. I felt like locking the door behind her and going upstairs to my room, but changed my mind when I turned to see Grandma watching me through the open dining room door. I gave Grandma a little wave then ran after Rumer down the driveway.

"Where are we going?" I asked, following as usual.

"To the beach, of course," she said.

She walked ahead of me, talking on her mobile and laughing every now and then. It was the happiest I had seen her since I'd arrived at Vinegar House.

There were two ways to access the beach at the bottom of the bluff. One way was to follow the road in a meandering path down to a sheltered area enclosed by tea-trees, then traipse through the dunes, until you reached the beach on the other side. This took at least 20 minutes on the way down and longer coming back up. The second way was to take a short cut down the beach access track that one of our long-dead relatives had hacked into the side of the bluff many years ago. This route only took five minutes, though the final section of path was inaccessible during high tide. It was also highly dangerous and forbidden by the adults.

At the end of the driveway, Rumer turned left towards the short route.

"Short cut?" I said.

"She won't know," said Rumer.

We looked back at the house. Someone was flapping a tablecloth out near the front door. We both turned right and took the long way down to the beach.

Rumer seemed back to her old self, chattering away about nothing much. I did notice there was no mention of a boyfriend, which was strange, as Rumer had been talking about boyfriends ever since she learned to speak.

"Are you still going out with Gerard?" I asked when she stopped talking long enough to take a breath.

"Gerard?" Her face was a question mark, then it cleared as she laughed and said, "Oh, Gerard. That was ages ago."

"So who is it now?" I was kicking a clod of earth down the path, so I wasn't really paying attention. When it took Rumer more than two seconds to answer, I looked up to see a strange expression on her face.

"No one," she said quickly. "I'm not seeing anyone at the moment."

I snorted.

"It's true," she said, with a toss of her head. "Not that it's any of *your* business. I've decided to concentrate on my studies this year."

This sounded like an Uncle Lawrence suggestion rather than an idea from Rumer.

"But you have someone in mind?" I guessed.

Her cheeks were flushed, though it could have just been the cold wind affecting them.

"Maybe," she said. "And is Isabella still a free agent?"

I nodded. I noticed she didn't ask me if I had a boyfriend. Probably thought I was too young. Or too ugly.

"Do you remember that time you tried to swim to Seal Rock?" she said with a laugh, one hand shielding her eyes as she looked out to sea.

"I wasn't trying to swim to Seal Rock," I said.

❋ ❋ ❋

I had tried to swim to Seal Rock a couple of months after Rumer had ruined my summer holiday at Ocean Side. The Harts needed to go to Port Eden for the weekend to check out a college for Megan, and Luke had resisted going along with them. Mum offered to take him with us to Vinegar House for the weekend. She seemed to think I would be pleased. Sometimes parents are so dense.

We left straight after school on the Friday. Dad was due to arrive later that night, something to do with work, which is why we had extra room in the car. I sat in the back, looking out the window, glad that Luke was a whole Oscar body width away from me. He and Oscar spent the trip going through Oscar's swap-card album. Luke tried talking to me a couple of times, but I had my earbuds in and pretended I couldn't hear him.

I expected things might get a little strange when Luke and Rumer met up again, but she greeted him as if they were old friends, and the moment passed smoothly. The twins, Angus and Lee, seemed glad to have another male ally. Uncle John and Aunty Wendy were arriving with their brood the next day and Isabella couldn't wait for Julia to get there.

That first night I went straight to bed after a dried out roast dinner – Mrs Skelton had excelled herself making sure that there was not even a drop of moisture left in the meat – claiming I had a headache. I could hear the thump and laughter of the others from the Blue Room. Probably playing Murder in the Dark, I thought, as I squeezed my eyes shut and willed sleep to come.

Uncle John and his family arrived by lunch the next day. Julia practically fell out of the car, grabbed onto Isabella and begged to be saved from her young brothers. The boys were totally out of control after their long journey. Aunty Wendy ushered the little ones into the kitchen for a treat, and Mum suggested the rest of us should take advantage of the good weather. Mrs Skelton had packed a picnic for us because the adults needed to talk business and wanted us out of the way. I didn't feel like going anywhere with Luke Hart, but there was no way I could get out of it without making it seem obvious. Rumer insisted on carrying the picnic basket and struggled earnestly, until Luke shyly sidled up to her and offered to take the basket from her. She brushed at a stray hair fallen over her face and thanked him as if that hadn't been her plan all along. I couldn't believe he could be so stupid – again.

No one talked about where we would go for lunch. We followed the driveway down to the bluff, ignored the DO NOT ENTER sign, then walked single file, carefully navigating the path down to the beach. Rumer was wearing ridiculous shoes without any tread which left her sliding over the tiny rocks that littered our way. When Luke offered her a helping hand I felt a pain like the thrust of a knife in my gut.

As I rounded the last bend on the path, I saw the beach spread out before us like a familiar friend. The bluff rocks that tumbled to the left and right of us held us in a horseshoe-shaped embrace. An old upturned dinghy which belonged to the house lay tethered on the sand like a turtle basking in the sun. The edge of the water was fringed with dirty foam that looked like something leftover from the Colonel's car washing efforts. And further out, much further, jutted a rock like the top of a submarine poking out from the waves. It was known as Seal Rock, though I'd never seen a seal basking on its smooth surface.

Once on the beach, Isabella laid out the tartan picnic rug, and Julia helped her unpack the food while I took off my shoes, rolled up my jeans and raced to check the rock pools. Limpets clung to the rock craters and a tiny crab scuttled into a crevice. In the largest pool I found a sea anemone, its feathery tentacles waving at my intrusive pokings. I yelled out to Isabella to come and look, but she waved her hand, too busy to hang out with me. I could feel Luke looking at me and I prayed that he wouldn't come over. Another part of me prayed that he would.

Angus and Lee had brought a ball along and were lobbing it to each other with exaggerated *ooohs* and *aaahs*. Rumer tried to join in, but her throws were pathetic short thrusts that dribbled over the wet packed sand. She laughed and held up her hands as if to say "I know, hopeless aren't I?" While I was silently agreeing with her, Luke strolled over, grabbed the ball, and leaned in close to instruct her on the finer points of throwing a ball.

The knife was jabbing into my gut again – little quick jabs of delicious pain that made no sense. I kicked at the sand and stubbed my toe on a submerged rock. Rumer's laughter added to my pain. I walked down to the water's edge to ease my throbbing toe. The water numbed my feet instantly, like I'd stepped in snow. I walked into the water a little further. Swimming at Bluff Beach was against the rules. Just like walking down the short cut path.

"Hey!" I had Luke's attention now. He was further up the beach. I looked back to see him cupping his hands to his lips and calling out to me. Rumer stood to one side behind him and shook her head at me. She said something to Luke, but her words were snatched away by a breeze that lifted the loose sand and dropped it swiftly again.

I didn't have to hear her words to know she was saying something about me. Maybe she was telling Luke I had a crush on him. The shame of the thought flooded through me like a hot tidal wave, so I did the only thing I could think of. I threw my windcheater off and ran further into the water. Although my feet were wet, it was nothing compared to the shock I felt as the water reached my knees. My shout of surprise was sucked from my body as a gritty wave dumped over me. I emerged to hear Isabella yelling at me, but I ignored her and began to swim away from the beach, my uneven strokes chopping at the steel-grey water. I hadn't planned to swim to Seal Rock, but it was something to aim for.

The cold was a band of ice squeezing tightly about my chest, leaving me gasping for breath. The water dragged at my jeans, which made it difficult to kick. I looked back at the shore and noticed Rumer standing alone to one side of the group I'd left behind. While the others were waving frantically, yelling at me to come back, Rumer was drawing something in the sand with a long piece of driftwood. She was clearly annoyed that I was getting all the attention for a change. I was smugly enjoying this thought when the next wave caught me from behind. It drew me into its frothy embrace, sucked me down and tumbled me around so that down became up, and up became sideways, tumbling, tumbling and the dull roar of it filled my ears. Then it spat me out, and I bobbed on the water's surface, gulping at the air, my heart racing, the blood pounding in my ears. It was time to return to the others.

And then I stepped off into nothing. The hard sand beneath my feet had fallen away into the deep water of the drop off. I tried a few wild strokes towards shore, but the tide held me fast in its grip. My feet frantically searched for solid ground, but I was treading water.

The first time I went under I was scared. I was going to die and the adults would find out I'd gone swimming and we would all get into trouble. I hoped Rumer would get into trouble the most. This is what I thought as the little silver bubbles of my breath rushed past me to the surface. I didn't know how, but in some way she was responsible for my unscheduled swim. She was definitely the reason Luke and I weren't friends any more. I clawed my way to the surface and managed two large gulps of air, waving my hand about before sinking again under the water. The cold was leaving my body. So had my mind. It wandered above the waves like a hovering seagull, watching the action around me. I could see the beach and those left ashore. I could see the craggy bluff with its jutting rocks and stunted coastal scrub. And further back, leaning over us all, was Vinegar House with its unfriendly face and crooked shingle roof.

That's when I noticed the light – a single beam of light reaching out to me from the very top window of Vinegar House. How strange, I thought.

And then someone grabbed my hair and dragged me to the surface, and I was back in my body again. I was hauled through the water then dumped, face first, on the smooth packed sand of the shore.

I gasped and coughed and coughed until a thin trickle of seawater left my mouth and then I started to cry. Isabella gathered me in her arms and shushed me, and told me off and shushed me again, until my sobs stopped and only hiccups remained.

My saviours – Angus and Luke – stood nearby, while the others crowded around in a huddle discussing what to do. If there was any possible way we could get back to Vinegar House and dry off without being detected, then that was our aim. An elaborate plan was hatched. A diversion. And it came from Rumer.

"Isabella should go up to the house and tell them I've twisted my ankle," she declared.

Somehow she'd managed to get the attention back onto her again.

"Then they'll know we've been down here," Lee argued.

"We'll go to the tree house," said Rumer. "The swimmers can go through the kitchen to the back stairs and dry off in the downstairs bathroom."

"But what if they ask about the others?" asked Julia.

"We'll say they've gone for a walk," said Rumer.

By now my teeth were chattering like a pair of castanets. It was a natty little beat that matched the knocking of my knees. Isabella looked at me and said, "All right."

I could feel Luke's eyes on me, but he didn't say anything. I wanted him to apologise to me, but I didn't know what for.

Isabella helped me into my windcheater, which stuck to my wet skin. Then Luke and Angus half-carried, half-dragged me back up the bluff path. We skirted around the back of the house, then the swimmers group broke off and headed to the kitchen door, while the others made their way to the tree house. I heard a single fake scream from Rumer before we entered the kitchen, and a minute later a babble of voices as people exited the front door. Angus grabbed a towel and headed for the Green Room to get dressed. Luke stood uneasily in the bathroom, and I shoved a towel into his hands.

"I'll use the bedroom," I said, gruffly.

"Hey, Shrimp, are you okay?"

His voice brought tears to my eyes, and they ran in two scalding rivers down my cheeks. He stepped towards me.

"I mean, that was just a crazy thing to do. You could've drowned or something—"

Crazy! Whatever I wanted to hear from him, it wasn't that.

"Shut up!" I hissed and I headed for the yellow bedroom.

I changed into some dry clothes and hoped no one would notice my change of outfit. Then I rubbed and rubbed at my hair until not a drop of water remained. Angus poked his head through the doorway to see how I was going.

"All done?" he asked.

I nodded.

"Let's keep this one quiet, Freya."

111

I nodded again. "Cross my throat and hope to choke," I said with the smallest of smiles. "Sorry–"

"Just save your next swim for summer. And not that beach."

Later that night, as we hung out in the Blue Room, I wondered how we'd gotten away with it. Everyone had been impressed with Rumer's skills as an actress. Except me, of course. She'd managed to cry on cue and had put up with a lot of fussing from the adults and an ugly bandage from Uncle Stephen (who may have been a doctor but whose triage skills were lacking). When she complained about her bandage, Luke fetched a tapestry cushion to elevate her foot. He had clearly forgotten there was nothing wrong with her. It made me want to scream.

Isabella had already thanked Rumer for saving the day. But I blamed Rumer. Somehow she'd forced me into the water. She'd nearly killed me and was now expecting my eternal thanks.

I played our favourite card game, Motors, but my heart wasn't in it. I flipped out the wrong cards or played out of turn and snapped at Lee when he nudged me with his foot. When Rumer asked me how I was feeling, I looked up to find Luke's eyes staring into mine. In the dim light, they were the slate grey of the sea, and I felt myself tumble and twist in their depths. I could feel the others judging me. I closed my eyes and felt the tumble once again as the waves crashed over me.

I heard the creak of a loose floorboard in the hallway, and we turned to the half-opened door to see Mrs Skelton walking past with our pile of wet towels.

For the rest of the night we waited to be summoned to the drawing room.

But nothing was ever said.

I'd tried to block that day from my mind, although whenever I looked under the Things I Hate About Rumer file I'd see it there. Rumer spent the next half an hour walking slowly up and down the hard sand talking to someone on her mobile. I sat and watched Seal Rock and wondered how I was going to survive my stay at Vinegar House. I didn't need to look back up the bluff to know that the house was leaning over me, somehow, filling me with dread. I checked my phone, but the only message was from my ex-friend Suzette Crompt, and I deleted it without even reading it.

Chapter 13

Do you know what it's like to want something so much that when you suddenly have it, well, it's hard to believe? I often wonder how Cinderella was so cool about the timely appearance of her godmother. I never quite believed that part of the story.

In my version – and I was always Cinderella, with Rumer being both of the ugly sisters and the wicked stepmother – the fairy godmother would appear but I could never be as cool as the real Cinderella was. I think it would be a little bit scary to have someone turn up like that.

I'm just not built for fairytale surprises. So when I pulled back the drapes the next morning and the first thing I saw was Luke Hart, I closed the drapes again and waited to hear the *brringgg* of a magic wand. And then I was going to have some harsh words to say to my fairy godmother for she was about two years too late. I peeked through the gap in the drapes to see Luke pushing a wheelbarrow up the long, winding driveway of Vinegar House, his breath fogging in the cold air. I considered I might still be dreaming in my sagging bed, but the cold snapping at my bare toes told me otherwise.

Luke Hart?

Here?

A wind was playing with the trees, bending them first one way then another, and it whistled through the gaps around the window. As I tried to recover from my shock at seeing Luke, he paused, wiped his brow, then looked directly up at the house. I stepped back from the curtains, paranoid that he had seen me in my PJs gazing out at him.

"Seems a waste of time, if you ask me," said Mrs Skelton from the doorway.

I hadn't heard my bedroom door open. Mrs Skelton had a way of creeping about that was unnerving. Something she'd learned from my grandmother, no doubt.

"I need to change the sheets," she continued. "It's Friday."

As if that explained everything.

"What's a waste of time, Mrs Skelton?" I asked. I pulled the heavy blankets from the bed and dumped them in a pile on the floor.

Mrs Skelton picked up the blankets and folded them neatly onto the armchair in the corner of the room. "Another gardener, with only us here to appreciate it. Not much of a garden anyway. But Mr Chilvers insisted, and what Mr Chilvers wants …" She pulled savagely at the top sheet, whipping it off in one move like a magician. "A waste of money, if you ask me."

I hadn't asked, but then that never stopped Mrs Skelton from telling people what she thought.

"How did Luke get here?" I asked.

Mrs Skelton shrugged. "Do you have any more washing?"

"I can do my own washing," I said, trying to be helpful.

She turned a sour face to me.

"Do you know how to use a washing machine?" she asked. "Your cousin just leaves her things on the floor."

"No. Really. It's fine."

"Suit yourself then." Her lips pressed together tightly, creases puckering around the edges as she gathered the sheets and pillowcases into her arms. "Good day for drying," she remarked as she left my room.

I moved to the heating coil underneath the window and tried to warm my numb fingers. Luke and Mr Chilvers were standing near the cubbyhouse tree, Mr Chilvers with an axe in one hand, while he gestured with the other.

"Not such a good day for chopping down trees," said Mrs Skelton, standing directly behind me, fresh sheets in her hands.

I think it pleased her when I jumped in fright.

"Why are they chopping that tree down?" I asked.

Mrs Skelton shrugged. "If you ask me, there're plenty of other things that need doing before chopping down that tree. This house is falling down around our ears. Still, that's men for you."

I had often wondered if there had ever been a Mr Skelton, or if the *Mrs* was just a social politeness. I couldn't imagine Mrs Skelton ever loving someone enough to marry them.

"But that's ours ... the cousins' tree house. They can't chop our tree down."

"Well, I don't know about that." Mrs Skelton dropped the linen onto the bed. "Looks like they've made up their mind."

"I'll make the bed." I wanted Mrs Skelton out of my room so I could get dressed. I was sure there'd been a mistake about the tree and I needed to talk to Mr Chilvers quickly.

"Suit yourself," she said, her eyes narrowed. "Your cousin never makes her bed. She—" Mrs Skelton checked herself, smoothed her apron, then nodded. "All right then."

I made my bed, then dressed in the clothes from the day before and barely stopped to brush my hair. I noticed a zit on my cheek as I looked in the mirror but there was no time to deal with it. I had a tree to save.

Luckily, nothing much had happened by the time I reached Mr Chilvers and Luke. They hadn't moved from the tree, though I noticed Mr Chilvers was still holding the axe. They both seemed caught up in their conversation.

"What are you doing?" I said, bluntly. I don't like confrontation. Have I told you that already? But even while my heart was pounding away in fright, my anger gave me the strength to stand my ground. "What are you doing to that tree?"

A part of me heard Luke's warm greeting, but I was too busy being outraged to care. I hadn't bothered much with the old tree since I'd arrived, but I knew it well. Knew its canopy in summer. Knew which limbs were good for climbing. I loved the way its roots pushed through the top of the soil and radiated out from the trunk like the thickened veins of an old man. This was a forever tree. And now they were going to chop it down.

"Hello," said Mr Chilvers. "Come to help?"

"You can't chop down that tree. You've … you've got no right–"

"Dieback," interrupted Mr Chilvers.

For a moment I thought he was telling me to get back or die.

"The tree's got dieback." He pointed to a large limb overhanging the driveway. "We need to take that off before it falls on someone."

"You're not cutting down the whole tree?" I asked, pointing to his axe.

He looked down at the axe as if surprised to see it in his hand.

"This is for Luke." He handed the axe to Luke. "We need some kindling chopped out the back. We'll deal with this another day. Come on, Luke," he said as he turned away from the tree.

I felt foolish, whining about a tree house as if I were a little kid. "Mrs Skelton said …"

Luke waited, but the beads of sweat on his forehead

and my need to reach up and wipe them away distracted me.

"How did you get here?" I asked instead.

"Got a lift with Mo."

Mo Phillips was a truck driver from town who had a reputation for having the messiest rig this side of the equator. The old Freya would have pumped Luke with questions about the trip, but I just scuffed at the ground.

"How's your grandmother?" he asked. "Have you heard from your parents?"

Luke Hart has the most amazing eyes that change colour – I kid you not. That day they were a dark blue. I was so busy being lost in their colour that I wasn't paying much attention to what he was saying.

"Nanna," I said automatically. "She's about the same. Happy to have Mum there though."

"How's life with Grandma Vinegar?" he said.

We used to laugh together about grandma's nickname. But I wasn't up for a cosy chat with Luke Hart. Not any more.

"What are you doing here?" I asked.

"Your grandmother offered me some work for the holidays," he said.

He pushed his fringe away from his face, and I

noticed the dirt trapped beneath his fingernails, his hands larger than I remembered.

"Really?"

"When I was here the other day. When we dropped you off."

"Oh." I tried to forget that Luke Hart had seen my sleep dribble during our trip to Vinegar House. "Where are you staying?"

"There's room at the cottage–"

"At the cottage? With Mr Chilvers?" I laughed. "How boring for you."

He looked down at his hands. "I'm saving for a car. So money's always handy. We don't all have rich relatives."

If Luke Hart had physically slapped me, it couldn't have hurt more. I remembered why I didn't want to talk to him any more. I didn't like feeling hurt. My mind was racing for a smart reply. Something really cutting that would stay with him for days to come. I was sure I'd have the perfect answer sometime tonight. Or maybe the next day. All I could manage right then was, "Right."

Luke touched me on the shoulder. "Freya–"

"Luke!" bellowed Mr Chilvers as he continued up the drive.

"Better not keep the boss waiting," I said.

Now *that* I was happy with.

Luke looked like he wanted to say something else, but then he turned and walked away. Movement from the attic window caught my attention, then a flash of light blinded me. I closed my eyes against it. When I opened them, the light was gone.

Chapter 14

Vinegar House has all the mod cons – you know – lukewarm and cold running water, a washing machine and even a clothes dryer which is practically like new because Mrs Skelton doesn't believe in wasting power.

Mrs Skelton insists on hanging clothes out on the washing line near the woodshed, even when it looks like it might rain. Half the time the clothes get a second rinse in a downpour. Still, it never stops her from taking it outside to dry. Which is how I found myself pegging out the washing that morning after my meeting with Luke and Mr Chilvers.

Rumer had actually made it for breakfast that morning. I'd told her about Luke working with Mr Chilvers, and she shrugged like she already knew.

"Could you help Mrs Skelton with the washing, girls?" asked Grandma Vinegar.

Of course, hanging out washing was high on my list of priorities for that day. Only to be outdone by my need to dust the library and polish the silver and maybe poke myself in the eye with a sharp stick.

Another one of my mother's sayings. I'd rather poke myself in the eye with a sharp stick …

Look, it doesn't matter. I never thought it was funny either.

Anyway, Grandma asked us to hang out the washing. It was more of a command than a question.

Rumer wrinkled her nose. "We just use the dryer at home," she said.

Grandma was buttering her piece of toast carefully right up to the edges. She did it in exactly the same way the Colonel did, and I spent some time wondering what strange little habits I'd picked up from my own parents.

"More money than sense," she quipped.

I never knew what to say when she came out with things like that, so I said, "Good eggs." And Grandma said, "Don't talk with your mouth filled with food, Freya. It's vulgar."

Rumer rose from the table and picked up her breakfast dishes.

"Don't forget the washing," reminded Grandma.

✳ ✳ ✳

Of course, Rumer had no intention of hanging out the washing, which is how I found myself lugging a basketload of sheets to the washing line by myself.

The sheets weren't like the ones we had at home. They were heavy-duty cotton sheets that had been made when Adam was a boy.

Another one of my mother's sayings.

The first sheet was hard enough. I had trouble getting it onto the line without trailing it in the dirt first. By the time I was ready for the second sheet, a wind had whipped up and the first wet sheet was slapping me in the face.

The thought of Luke was like a toothache. I knew it was going to hurt to go there, but I kept going back to probe and poke. I was probing my Luke tooth as I dealt with the washing, trying to imagine what I might say to him if he appeared from out of nowhere.

I reverted to some of my favourite Luke Hart daydreams – the ones I used to have before I realised I didn't really like him that much any more.

Luke Hart was walking up the garden path dressed in his riding pants and white shirt. He was wet through after having fallen into the lake ...

No, wait. That was Mr Darcy.

Luke and I were running towards each other on Bluff

Beach. The world was in slow motion. I was wearing a white sundress. Even though I don't own a white sundress because white really isn't my colour. It was kind of old fashioned and long and wet on the hem where it had trailed in the waves. Amazingly, I was tanned, and the zit on my left cheek had miraculously disappeared—

The *slap slap* of wet sheets ended that thought.

I was Juliet, and Luke was my Romeo, and I was wearing a floaty kind of dress, not white this time, and my hair was more blond than the horrible nothing-brown that it really is, and Luke was wearing his gardening work boots ...

I hated that story. Two dumb kids who died for nothing.

Slap, slap, wet pillowcase.

I dreamed that Luke Hart marched into the dining room at Vinegar House at dinnertime, pulled me from my chair, and kissed me right then and there in front of Grandma Vinegar and Rumer and Mrs Skelton. I imagined the shock on their faces. I imagined the shock on mine. The clatter of cutlery as Grandma gasped and dropped them in dismay. The shatter of broken glass as Rumer's drink slipped from her fingers. And Mrs Skelton saying, "That boy really loves that girl, if you ask me."

Slap, slap, another wet pillowcase.

I imagined – and this was one of my favourite imagines, so I tried not to use it too much – I imagined that I had become incredibly ill due to the poor cooking skills of Mrs Skelton and the excessive taking of air that Grandma Vinegar had insisted on. I had caught a chill and had to take to my bed. Luke Hart rushed to my side and declared his undying love; that it was me he had loved all along, and Rumer had just been a distraction. And then–

That's when I noticed that Luke was watching me standing at the washing line getting slapped by wet washing. I wondered how long he'd been watching me. I wondered which particular drama he had arrived at. My body went hot and cold and hot all over as I wondered what I had actually been doing.

Between you and me, sometimes I can get quite involved in my daydreams. I have sometimes caught myself acting out a part or murmuring dialogue aloud. I was hoping Luke Hart hadn't caught me doing anything strange like that.

Luke was holding a second basketload of washing and he was looking at me with a frown on his face.

"What are you doing?" he asked when he realised that I was watching him watch me.

I pointed to the washing line that was now sporting

sheets and pillowcases and a threadbare tablecloth. "Making pancakes," I said.

Luke placed the basket down at my feet. He ignored my sarcasm.

"Were you talking to someone?" he asked.

"No."

Slap, slap, a pillowcase to the face.

"You were talking," he said. "I saw you. And you were kind of …" He moved his arms about as if unsure about what to say.

"I'm in a play," I said.

I was pleased with my answer. It was a great answer. I wasn't usually so quick with great answers.

And then he asked, "What play?"

"What play?" I grabbed a tea towel from the second basket. "The school play, of course. I'm rehearsing my lines."

"Oh. Great," said Luke. "Good on you. It's just … I didn't think you were into that sort of thing. I mean like–"

"Like Rumer?" By now I had used ten pegs on one tea towel.

"No. Yes. I thought more like your sister. She's into all that stuff, isn't she?"

"Isabella? Yes, well, we do share the same genes."

I was pretty sure this was true. We weren't up to genes yet in biology.

"So what part are you playing?" he asked.

"Part?"

"In the school play. It's *Romeo and Juliet*, isn't it?"

I didn't even know there was a real school play.

"Yes, that's right. It's just a small part. Only a couple of lines."

I only knew two characters from *Romeo and Juliet*.

1. Romeo

2. Juliet.

"The fight scenes were pretty cool," said Luke. "Hard to understand what they were saying sometimes. Stupid ending though."

"It's a classic!" I said hotly.

He shrugged. "So give me some lines."

"What?"

"Go on. Practise your lines on me."

"I … I …" I stamped my foot.

I don't know about you, but I find that when I am really embarrassed, the best reaction is anger. It's much better than crying because then people feel sorry for you, and I don't want to be pitied. So that's why I let Luke have it.

"You can't boss me around any more, Luke Hart.

And you're … you're—"

"Luke!" It was Mr Chilvers from down at the woodshed.

I grabbed a sheet from the basket and tried to drape it over the line, but the wind picked it up and threw it back into my face, then onto the ground. I almost heard the *brringgg* of my fairy godmother's wand. She was obviously in a bad mood today. I let out a low growl when Luke moved forwards to help me.

"Look what you've done," I said. "This is all your fault."

"Shrimp—"

"Don't call me that! Shrimp was a little kid – somebody you used to know. You don't know me. And don't pretend—"

"Luke!"

Mr Chilvers was lugging a barrowload of mulch and nodding at Luke to follow him.

Luke picked the sheet up off the ground. He placed it gently into the empty washing basket.

He took my face in his hands and looked deeply into my eyes in a way he had never looked at me before. And then he leaned in and we locked lips tighter than the seal on the hatch of a diving submarine, his thumb gently brushing away a tear that had rolled down my cheek …

I really had to stop daydreaming about someone who didn't even exist.

The real Luke left me standing at the washing line.

The sheet was still on the ground.

Luke followed Mr Chilvers to the vegetable patch without a backward glance.

And I didn't need to look behind me to feel Vinegar House frowning down on us.

"Oh, shut up," I said.

Chapter 15

The attic had always been out of bounds to the grandchildren. Dad told me there was nothing up there anyway, just some old stuff that nobody had bothered to throw away. But Isabella and I had spent hours imagining all kinds of things: ancient treasure maps and toys, wedding dresses and telephones with dial-up numbers. We'd even asked once or twice if we could just look and not touch anything, but Grandma Vinegar insisted that it was no place for nosey children and we'd probably just get ourselves injured or incredibly dirty. I got the feeling that the idea of dirt was the thing that affected her the most.

There were other rooms in Vinegar House locked against prying eyes, but they never held the same appeal as the attic. Mrs Skelton was the keeper of the keys. She wore them on a crocheted chain around her neck, along with another chain that held her reading glasses. This meant she had access to any of the locked doors at Vinegar House whenever she wished. Some days I'd catch a glimpse of a normally locked up room through a half-opened door as Mrs Skelton ran her duster over unused furniture or opened a window to let air into the room. Grandma Vinegar was very big on fresh air. She was always telling us to go outside and get some air into our lungs, as if the house didn't have enough oxygen to spare.

And then one day I had my chance. It was the day after the *washing line incident*, as I had labelled it in my head. As I left my bedroom to go downstairs for lunch, I noticed a shaft of light at the end of the corridor where there shouldn't have been one. I wondered if the blackbirds had made their way through to the ceiling. Mrs Skelton had been complaining that the birds had made a nest in the eaves, and that Mr Chilvers needed to find out where they were getting in and board it up. But of course, because Mrs Skelton was complaining about it, Mr Chilvers was taking his time getting around to fixing the problem.

I hurried past the bathroom door. As I walked past Rumer's bedroom there was the faint sound of a keyboard being tapped. Further down the hall I realised that the shaft of light was spilling down the tiny flight of stairs which were usually out of bounds.

The door to the attic was open. I stopped at the foot of the stairs and listened, but there were no sounds from above. Mrs Skelton must have left the door open accidentally. She was probably on her way back right now to close it. Even as I was thinking this, I climbed the stairs, the sun shaft like a beckoning finger that I couldn't resist. The stairs were quite steep, the boards narrow as if made for tiny feet. At the top there was a small landing and the half-opened door. I pushed it fully open and walked into the forbidden space.

I was disappointed.

The attic was spotless. No cobwebs hung from the ceiling. No mountains of treasure were piled up high. There were boxes. Plenty of boxes. Some looked like boxes that tinned food might come in. Others looked older, like tea-chests, or wooden-slatted things, dark with age. In one corner sat a stack of old suitcases with brass corners and tarnished locks. A scrap of material peeked out from one suitcase, so I figured it might hold old clothes. And there, solving the mystery of the missing piece of furniture from the Blue Room, was the floor-length mirror.

The window was at shoulder-height and the outside was speckled from years of sea spray. It was octagonal in shape and dusty inside, apart from a spot in the

134

centre that looked as if someone had cleared it recently for a better view. I didn't remember ever seeing the window from outside. The overhanging eaves may have had something to do with this, or it could have been that I never bothered to look up that high. I imagined children dressed in old-fashioned clothes playing marbles or hide-and-seek up here. Had anyone peered from this window waiting for the arrival of a horse and cart? Had someone watched a sailing ship glide through the grey water beyond the bluff?

I could see the edge of the sweeping driveway and the bluff rocks that surrounded us. The water was white-capped today, a hectic motion created by the wind which whistled through the gap in the window's lintel. Sunlight poured weakly through the window, hitting the mirror that had been propped up against a wardrobe just opposite the stairs.

"What are you doing?"

I fell against the window in fright and looked around to see Rumer peering in at me from the doorway.

"The attic," I said simply. "I've never been in here before."

"Boring, isn't it," she said. "Daddy showed me up here once." She wandered about the room, sniffing once. She wrinkled her nose then sighed. "This is the worst holiday ever. You'd better come down for lunch. I am not going down there by myself."

As we left, a wooden chest caught my eye. Its curved lid was tied down with leather straps, each strap secured by a rusted buckle. I touched it briefly as I left the room, and it seemed warm to my fingers. As I passed the mirror I thought I caught a glimpse of blond hair in its cracked corner, but when I took a closer look there was just the reflection of the door. Even as I decided I had seen Rumer's reflection as she left the room I shivered a little.

I made sure the door was ajar at the same angle I'd found it, and followed Rumer down the stairs. By the time I reached the main staircase, I looked back to the attic stairs, but the shaft of light had disappeared and the end of the corridor was in shadow.

And somewhere above us I heard the attic door slam shut.

Chapter 16

Have you ever noticed that there are some things people say that usually mean the opposite of what they are saying?

Like, when someone says, "To be perfectly honest," I doubt that's what they're being.

Or, "I don't want to alarm you," means that they're just about to scare you to death.

Or, "With all due respect," means they have no respect for you at all, and they're just about to be very rude.

So when Mrs Skelton goes around saying, "If you ask me," it's usually because she knows that no one is going to ask her, so she's going to tell you anyway.

I was thinking about this after lunch that same day when Mrs Skelton sent me to look for Mr Chilvers because he hadn't done something she'd asked him to do, and now his life wasn't worth living, *if you asked her.*

"And tell him Mrs Kramer is very unhappy," she added as I left.

Why don't you tell him yourself? I thought. But I just nodded and slammed the door behind me. I hoped I wouldn't come across Luke. Just the thought of the stupid wet sheets and my tantrum made the breath catch in my throat.

Outside, the air tasted like a crisp Granny Smith apple, all tart and juicy. I could hear the *thunk-thunking* of an axe at work. Mr Chilvers was obviously down at the woodshed, which is why I took the path that led to the front of the house. Mr Chilvers could wait; I had a sudden urge to visit the tree house.

I couldn't remember the last time I'd climbed up to the tree house. My feet reached for familiar footholds, but I felt awkward and out of practice. By the time I reached the platform I was puffing like an old goat. If I looked behind me, I could see Vinegar House all dark and brooding, smoke trailing from the kitchen chimney. Ahead of me lay the sea. Several large gulls coasted about on the air currents above the bluff.

A few plastic figures – like the ones you find in a fast-food kid's meal – were all that remained from our elaborate tree house days when we'd drag cushions and blankets and toys up to the platform.

"Hello?" came a voice from below.

I stayed still and peered through the branches, barely daring to breathe. It was Luke. I wondered if he'd go away if I ignored him.

"Freya?"

"Oh. Hi!" I moved slightly so he could see my face.

"How's the view?" He was pretending that nothing had happened. Pretending that he wasn't embarrassed by my recent lunatic rantings.

"Good. Great. You should try it sometime," I babbled.

The next thing I knew, the tree was shaking as Luke clambered up.

"I didn't mean ... oh, there you are," I continued.

Luke's face appeared first, then he hitched himself up to sit beside me.

"You're right," he said, settling in. "It is a good view. So give me the guided tour."

Luke Hart was sitting next to me, and he smelled like burning leaves and hand soap and chewing gum. It was the most heavenly thing I had ever smelled in my life. And that included the smell of vanilla and baking bread.

I had never thought of a tree house scenario before, and mentally added it to my list of Luke Hart daydreams.

"Okay," I said, pointing towards the coastline. "To the right is Homsea. You can't see it from here, but if you followed the coastline all the way around you'd eventually bump into the Homsea Jetty."

"Check."

"To the left of us is the bluff. It gets in the way of us seeing any further, but if you swam along the coastline on the left, you'd come to Craddock's farm."

"Check. Look, sorry about that, er …" he said. "I don't know what I said—"

I wondered what he was apologising for, then I realised he didn't know either. I interrupted him. "And straight ahead is Seal Rock. And just past that … I think that's a boat."

"What?"

"I think there's a boat." I pointed out to where I was looking. "A speedboat."

Luke leaned in closer to follow the direction of my finger. "I can't see anything," he grumbled.

His voice was so close to my ear that the words sent a shock wave through me. I wanted him to speak again.

"I'm pretty sure there's a boat," I insisted.

"Are you cold?" he asked.

I hadn't realised I was trembling, but it wasn't the cold weather making my body shake.

"A little," I said.

"Do you want my coat?" he asked.

"No!" I didn't want him to move away.

He grabbed my pointing hand and sandwiched it between his own two hands.

"Is that better?" he asked.

I could barely nod. I'd stopped breathing and everything about that moment was like stumbling into a 3-D movie after living a 2-D life. The rough planks of the tree house were hard against my back. I could hear the screech of the gulls as they squabbled on Bluff Beach and, further out, the faint drone of the speedboat, which was nearly out of sight. The skin on Luke's hands was rough but his touch was gentle, and he held my hand carefully as if it might break.

"Freya!" Mrs Skelton's voice rose into the thin winter air and life returned to 2-D.

I took a breath and giggled nervously.

"I need to go. Got an errand," I explained.

"I'll go first," Luke offered, letting go of my hand. "I'll make a nice soft landing for you if you fall."

As I waited for Luke to climb down out of my way, I spied a folded piece of paper poking out from between two overlapping wood planks. It was shoved in so tightly that I tore it a little as I pulled it out. Inside only one word was scrawled in untidy writing.

Murderer.

A left over note, probably, from one of our many games of Murder in the Dark.

"Are you right?" called out Luke.

I shoved the note into my pocket. Then I scrambled down the tree, conscious that Luke was watching my every move.

❋ ❋ ❋

I walked down the garden path to the stump behind the woodshed where Mr Chilvers was splitting logs. I stood for a moment, unsure what to do, and noticed the way his shirtsleeves were rolled back and the sweat patches that had formed at his armpits. I'd never spent much time thinking about Mr Chilvers, but when I had it was to think of him as an old man. Perhaps it was the grey at his temples or the work overalls he wore that had encouraged this idea, but I realised that he was probably younger than my father. Definitely older than Luke Hart. Not that I was thinking about him …

Mr Chilvers paused in his chopping and started when he looked up to find me watching him.

"Mrs Skelton told me to ask you—"

He waved his hand, cutting me off. "I know what she wants," he said. "And I'll get to it. But there's more bad weather coming, and Mrs Kramer will want that fire in the dining room running full pelt. And I don't fancy chopping wood in the rain."

I looked to the woodshed that was stacked to the roof with logs, but if he noticed my gaze he ignored it.

"Mrs Skelton is unhappy, I mean—"

"Mrs Skelton isn't happy unless she's unhappy with someone," he noted as he grabbed an armful of logs and stacked them neatly against the outside wall of the shed.

"She said to tell you that Mrs … Grandma is very unhappy," I repeated dutifully. "Sorry," I added, just so he would realise I was only the messenger.

"So Mrs Kramer is very unhappy that I haven't fixed a loose shelf in the pantry? More like Mrs Skelton is unhappy." He cocked an eyebrow at me and gave me a wry smile.

"Anyway," I shuffled about scuffing at the ground, "that was the message."

Mr Chilvers picked up the axe to inspect its edge.

I wondered why a man like Mr Chilvers would hide himself away in the middle of the end of nowhere looking after a property that was clearly falling down around his ears for an old lady who didn't appreciate it.

"Why do you work here?" I asked suddenly. I hadn't meant to ask the question aloud and I felt embarrassed.

"It suits me." He continued inspecting the axe head for nicks.

"What did you do before you worked here?"

He sighed. "You can tell Mrs Skelton if she wants information, she can ask me herself."

"No, no, I–"

"So, not Mrs Skelton?"

I shook my head.

He pulled out his handkerchief, blew his nose, then shoved the tatty material back into his overall's pocket.

"I used to work a farm not too far from here. Been in our family for three generations. We had a couple of bad years. Then a couple more. My wife wanted to quit it, but ..." He shrugged his shoulders. "She left. She took the kids, and I stayed on. I was just hanging out for one good year. The bank took it in the end. They took everything."

I didn't know what to say.

"All that hard work, and they just swooped in like a pack of vultures," he continued. "None of them ever done an honest day's work in their life. Just had to look at their hands to know that."

I looked at Mr Chilvers's own hands, which were blunt and scarred.

"Still, nothing good comes from profiting at the expense of others." He looked up at Vinegar House.

"What do you mean?" I followed his gaze. There was a figure at the kitchen window but I couldn't tell who it was from so far away.

Mr Chilvers picked up fallen bark from around the chopping block and threw it into a small metal bucket hanging from the shed wall.

"Mr Chilvers?"

"You can tell Mrs Skelton I'll fix her shelf after lunch."

A gust of wind sprang up from nowhere, pushing hair into my face as I watched Mr Chilvers prepare to leave. I wanted to ask him what he meant by profiting at the expense of others. I wanted to ask what he knew about my family, but it seemed disloyal somehow to be asking a stranger.

"Do you still see them?" I asked instead. "Your children?"

He raised the axe and I flinched, thinking of the folded over paper in my pocket.

Murderer.

Then he swung it into the chopping block with such

force that it drove a split in the wood. "A couple of times a year," he said. "That's all I can manage. They've got a new dad now, so I don't want to … you know … mess things up for them."

I suddenly wanted to talk to my own dad, so I mumbled something and turned back to the house, the wind gusting around my body, pushing me this way and that. There was a prickle at my neck, and I knew that if I turned around I would see Mr Chilvers watching me. But when I finally did turn to look back at the kitchen door, he was nowhere in sight.

Chapter 17

Mum sounded happier when I talked to her later that day. She was still worried, but Nanna was doing much better on new medication. When the Colonel got on to the phone I forgot how much I'd wanted to hear his voice. He wanted to know how my homework was going, had I heard from Isabella and was I pulling my weight with chores around Grandma's house. I ended our conversation with, "Good to hear from you too" even though he hadn't said that. I got a grumpy reply, then I was handed back to Mum.

"I think that's the doorbell," I heard her say. Obviously, she was trying to get Dad out of the room. "Freya, please be patient with your father, he really does miss you."

"Uh-huh."

"Freya!"

"Sorry, Mum."

"You know that's just his way."

Grandma Vinegar paused at the library door to see me perched on the arm of the big reading chair. "Please sit on the chair properly, Freya. The armrest is for arms. Thus its name."

"Grandma sends her love, Mum," I said, moving onto the seat of the chair.

Grandma Vinegar glared at me suspiciously.

"I've gotta go now. Give my love to Nanna." I hung up. "Mum says hello."

"And how is everything there?"

"Good. Nanna's doing well. Everyone's well," I said.

Grandma nodded once. "I thought we could all watch a movie tonight," she said.

Luckily I was sitting down, because if I'd been standing, I would have fallen over. It was like … it was like Grandma was trying to be nice to me.

"It's a favourite of mine, with Fred Astaire. He was the best dancer to ever come out of Hollywood. Although Gene Kelly was also a very good dancer."

Then again, maybe not. Fred Astaire? I'd never heard of the guy. And who was Gene whatsit?

"That's something to look forward to," I said.

Her eyes narrowed.

"I mean, I love musicals. So does Rumer. We'll both be there. It's a date," I babbled. There was no way

148

Rumer was going to get out of this torture.

Grandma sniffed. "Straight after dinner," she said.

"Great," I said.

Great.

Ffffantastic.

❋ ❋ ❋

The three of us cosied up in the TV room after dinner. This was the smallest of the downstairs rooms – smaller than the library even – but it still had its own fireplace, which sported a fire that Mr Chilvers had built up so much that the room was nearly hot. Grandma turned on the TV and found the right channel. She'd invited Mrs Skelton along, but the housekeeper said she had plenty of things to do before she got to bed that night. She said it in that way that meant everyone watching TV was a burden to her, and she just wanted us to know it. I'm not sure that Grandma received the message, but if she did, she hid it well.

Rumer had hidden her mobile under the cushion on her lap and was texting secretly before the opening credits had even rolled. It was an ancient movie – black and white – and it was pretty silly really. Lots of snappy talking. Misunderstandings. Dancing and singing. But there was a point during the movie where the main guy was trying to tell the girl he loved how he thought about her day and night – and I got it.

It's not that I planned to think about Luke Hart. It's just that he popped into my head all the time. I could not stop thinking about Luke Hart, and there was nothing I could do about it.

Near the end of the movie the power dropped out as it did sometimes, and we bumped around in the dark.

"There's the power gone again. Could you get a candle from the kitchen, Freya?" said Grandma. "Rumer, you'll find a torch in the library."

Grandma was still giving Rumer instructions as I groped my way out of the TV room, across the entry hall, and into the kitchen. There was always a candle next to the stove, but it took me a while to find the matches. As I was fumbling about in the dark I had the feeling that someone was watching me. I moved over to the window, which was a paler grey in the dark, but there was no moon that night – nothing to help me see what I was doing. I struck a match and lit the candle, then raised it up before me to see a face at the window.

Just a face.

A scream stuck in my throat and I clung to the windowsill for support as I felt faint, then there was a tapping at the window and I had a closer look and realised it was Mr Chilvers dressed in dark clothes. After several deep breaths I went to the back door, unlocked it and he stood in the doorway.

"Just checking everything's all right up here," he said. "The power's out at the cottage."

"Here too," I said. "But we're fine."

He nodded once, then turned away and I locked the door behind him.

Back in the TV room, Rumer had found two torches and was waiting impatiently for me.

"Hurry up," she said.

Rumer handed a torch to Grandma who told us to go to bed, that she would be right up. Then Rumer pushed me out of the way as we reached the top of the stairs and she headed for the bathroom. By the time I reached my bedroom, I heard the satisfied slam of the bathroom door and the click of the lock and I felt that familiar fizz of anger towards her.

That's when I noticed a square of pale colour poking out from under the gap beneath Rumer's door. Without thinking about it, I grabbed it – it felt like paper – then went to my room and shut the door with such a force that the draft snuffed my candle out. I fumbled my way over to the uncovered window but couldn't really see anything. I shoved it under my pillow, then went to sleep.

Chapter 18

I waited until morning to read the note, but it only confirmed what I already knew – that the romance between Luke and Rumer was back on. I think I'd known that first hug between them when Mrs Hart dropped me off at Vinegar House. I knew it like I knew that fishing off the Homsea Jetty during high tide was the best time for squiding; like I knew Miss Maudy's shop smelled of mothballs and the linseed oil rubbed into its wooden flooring; like I knew Rudy Heinrich would be eating a Danish at 11 am every work day while he pointed his radar gun at passing traffic. It was a fact. And they were doing it under my very nose. They had probably planned it all along, but they hadn't reckoned on me being at Vinegar House for the holidays. Rumer's closed bedroom door suddenly made sense. She was probably slipping out to meet Luke while pretending to be holed up in her room.

I'd been thinking about Luke night and day, and now I just felt stupid.

The front of the wrinkled envelope was marked with the letter R in a broad, fat capital. It didn't look at all like an F. It had been under Rumer's door. I knew it was wrong for me to open it, because I couldn't even pretend that it was meant for me. I was thinking this even as I lifted the flap on the envelope and pulled out the note that was short and to the point.

Dear R,

I watched you last night through your bedroom window. You remind me of an angel. I know you're not. I can hear you laughing as you read this now.

I know you don't want to see me. You've made that clear. But it's not that easy. I can't turn off how I feel. Not like you.

I know I should hate you.

But I can't.

L xx

I was feeling a little dizzy. I read the note again and then one more time. I slipped it back into the envelope and then hid it at the back of the dresser drawer. I avoided looking in the mirror. I was scared to think what I might see.

✳ ✳ ✳

Sunday mornings at home are kind of special. Even the Colonel makes an effort, firing up the hotplate for a cooked breakfast with minimal growling. If Isabella is home, Oscar wakes her up then we all sit down at the table and discuss what's happened that week. The dog is allowed inside and sits under the table for scraps. Mum's a kinder teacher, so she usually has a funny story about one of the little kids. Dad talks about the chores he has set himself up for that day, though few of them ever get done. Oscar is big on jokes, so there's usually a hundred knock knock jokes until we bribe him to stop. Isabella always talks about some show she's seen in town, or some of the books she's been reading. Her and Mum are mad readers, so they always try and outdo each other in the reading stakes.

And me? I like to sit there and let it all wash over me, like the gentle lapping of the incoming tide. It's my second-favourite place to be, after the jetty, of course. There's usually some music going on in the background, and in the old days, the Harts might have dropped over for a muffin or a pancake or a cup of freshly ground coffee that always smelled better than it tasted.

Sunday morning was like every other morning at Vinegar House.

I'd woken up early to a cold hot water bottle. I read the note, several times, then shoved it into my dresser. Then onto a quick hot shower in the downstairs bathroom to melt the icicles off my nose. I'd just finished dressing when Mrs Skelton came in and made my bed. I stood in front of the dresser, fussing around as if I had something to hide.

I decided it was a good day to do my homework. I needed to stay out of Rumer's way and I definitely didn't want to see Luke. I'd read the note so many times that I'd memorised it by heart. I wondered when Luke had slipped it under Rumer's door, though it would have been easy enough when we were watching the movie together. I kept out of Grandma's way, for whenever she saw me she'd tell me to go out and take some air. (I don't know where I was supposed to take it.) But Luke was outside, so I stayed inside, prowling around the hallways of Vinegar House, peering into cupboards that held ancient linen and tarnished silver, gazing into the eyes of long-dead relatives – dusty oil portraits in the library, which smelled of wood ash and mildewed books – and occasionally checking the door to the attic, which remained locked.

I dreamed of Mum's cooking. Mrs Skelton's food was beige. No matter what vegetable she touched, she cooked it for so long that she managed to leach all colour from it. We had potatoes at every main meal, with meat and one other vegetable, which could be beans or carrots or broccoli or peas. Our main meal was in the middle of the day with a light dinner at five o'clock. This often had me hunting for food late at night when the others were in bed and the fire was burning low in the drawing room grate.

I'd offered to cook when I first arrived at Vinegar House, hoping to add some excitement to the menu, but Mrs Skelton seemed so cross with the idea that I didn't bother. Instead, I was allowed to help her, which meant not doing very much at all. It was during one of these sessions that I asked Mrs Skelton about the attic.

Mrs Skelton and I were preparing the food for Sunday lunch. We were sitting at the kitchen table, a low, wide pine thing that she polished every night with a layer of beeswax. A gleaming new stove stood beside the faithful wood range that belched smoke whenever the wind blew down the chimney. The new stove had been a present from the family, but Mrs Skelton preferred to use the wood range, with its ancient thermometer set in the oven door and the plate racks above the hotplate where she could warm the dinner plates. Through the kitchen window I had a good view of the woodshed and, further down the path, the gardener's cottage where a thin wisp of smoke hung about the aerial on the low roof. I imagined Mr Chilvers and Luke settled in at night, watching TV with dinner on their laps instead of having to sit up at a table in a stuffy dining room for a light meal. I wondered what they talked about all day. I wondered if Luke ever mentioned me.

"Was the attic always the attic?" I asked the housekeeper as I peeled a potato larger than my hand.

She peered at me. "Well, it was never the basement," she said, slicing away a sliver of fat from a rolled piece of beef.

I laughed, thinking she'd made a joke, but she concentrated on her task without smiling. The clock on the kitchen dresser added a slow tick in the background and a breeze rattled the window. Mrs Skelton mumbled something about a certain person not doing his job properly as she stabbed viciously at the meat. Mr Chilvers was always in her bad books.

"I mean, was it ever someone's bedroom?" I persisted.

"Not while I've lived here," she said, turning the

meat and slicing again. "There are enough rooms in this house without needing to use that as a bedroom, if you ask me."

I grabbed another potato. "I guess." I felt the housekeeper's eyes on me. "Still, it would make a cool bedroom. It has such a great view." I realised my mistake as soon as the words left my lips. As far as Mrs Skelton knew, I had never been up to the attic. "I mean … I imagine the view would be good. Cause it's up high."

I looked up to see Mrs Skelton pointing her knife at me. "The eyes," she said.

I watched her grab the potato out of my hand then dig away at some small indents. "Second-rate potatoes at first-rate prices," she muttered. "That's what you get for buying from The Horn."

The Horn was the vegetable shop in Homsea. As far as I knew, Mum had never had any complaints about the quality of its potatoes.

I wiped my hands and made an excuse to leave.

"If there's something you want to ask, then ask it," said Mrs Skelton. "I'll either have an answer for you or I won't." She was working away at the potato, a few stray wisps of hair waving about her face.

"Why can't I go in the attic? I won't hurt anything."

Mrs Skelton added the potato to a bowl of water.

"When I was your age I was earning a living," she said, covering the bowl with a checked tea towel.

This was no answer. I sighed and stood up to leave.

"There's nothing up there for you. Just a whole lot of old things that need throwing away, if you ask me. Or a few that need airing out to the world. But, your grandmother won't hear of it. And she won't want you poking around up there."

A memory of light pulsing from the attic window flashed into my mind, and I wondered why. Why think of that now? I had a sudden urge to go upstairs and check that Rumer's note was still tucked away in my drawer.

I watched Mrs Skelton add some fat to a baking tray, then place the meat onto the tray. I thought it was strange that she had bothered to trim the fat from the meat when she had planned to roast it in fat all along. I watched the house keys, on the crocheted chain about her neck, swing over the pan.

"If you really want to help, there are library shelves that need attention," she said. "You need to pull out the books to give it a good dust. I usually start at the bottom and work my way up."

And with that she handed me a rag and shooed me out of the kitchen.

* * *

When I went upstairs later to get Rumer for lunch, there was another envelope under her door. As I wondered what to do, I heard footsteps approaching the door from inside her room, then the door swung open and Rumer stood before me.

"What?" she demanded.

"Mrs Skelton says to come down for lunch," I said.

"I'll be there in a minute," she said, then shut the door in my face.

It wasn't until I walked away that I noticed I had the note concealed carefully in my hand. I didn't remember picking it up. I went straight to my room and closed the door behind me. There was the same R on the envelope. I didn't bother to open it but put it into my dresser drawer then went downstairs for lunch. And all the time it was like I was watching myself do this. It was like watching a movie.

And the lead character was making no sense.

Chapter 19

I wasn't surprised that Luke and Rumer had got together again, but it did make me feel alone in a way I'd never felt alone before. Obviously, they'd had a fight, but that was typical of Rumer. She'd get over it and everything would be sweet until she changed her mind again.

I am not a bad person. If you ever told me your deepest darkest secret, I wouldn't tell anyone. If you gave me your most precious thing to care for, I would care for it. If you wanted the truth, I would give it to you.

So, I'd like to tell you that I handed the notes over to Rumer and confessed to everything. Or even that I'd slipped them back under her bedroom door. But I did neither of these things. Instead the notes lay in my drawer, a guilty secret that made my heart race just with the sheer thought of it. Maybe it was guilt that woke me in the early hours of the following morning.

Every house has its own sounds in the dark hours. Our shack at Ocean Side has a tin roof that *tick-ticks* as it cools down after a hot summer's day. At home I can usually hear the Colonel snoring from his bedroom or the dog scratching fleas as he sleeps outside my door. Vinegar House has its own dark hour noises. There's the grandfather clock that stands in the entry hall and chimes the arrival of every new quarter hour. The hissing of possums as they scurry over the roof. The creaks and sighs and groans as the house settles its bones after a hard day's work. And then there is the rattling of the windows during windy nights and the never-endingness of the waves beating themselves up against the bluff.

I'm not sure which noise woke me at 2.47 am the next morning. All I know is that one moment I was dead asleep and the next my eyes were wide open and I was checking the clock on my mobile. There was something about the time that bothered me, then I realised it was the same time I'd woken nights before. I lay in bed for a while listening to the waves break below the bluff. I wanted to be home. I wanted to leave Rumer and Luke to whatever game they were playing and Mrs Skelton and her horrible food and Grandma Vinegar and her grumpy ways.

I hadn't eaten much of Mrs Skelton's light dinner. We'd had something she called mock fish – grated potato and flour pressed into a patty and fried up. She'd served it with a light salad and, strangely, boiled potatoes – just in case we didn't have enough potato on our plate. The patty didn't taste like anything much except maybe half-raw potato and uncooked flour. I'd poked at it and moved it around my plate. The salad was limp with too much dressing. I picked at the potatoes, which had been boiled so long that they fell apart like floury clods of earth. In bed, at 2.53, my stomach rumbled as I thought of fresh bread from the pantry. Mrs Skelton made her own, and it was the one thing she was good at. I grabbed my mobile, turned on the torch app, slipped on a windcheater, and made my way to the bedroom door without bumping into anything. As I stepped out of my room I noticed silvery light spilling down the attic stairs.

The attic door was open.

My heart skipped a beat as I stood and considered my options.

1. Return to bed, forget about the pantry, and wait until breakfast to fill my stomach.

2. Go downstairs and make a sandwich, then go straight back to bed. Or …

3. Go to the attic and have another look around while the door was open.

I decided on the pantry. I began to plan the filling for my sandwich – maybe bread and cheese, or some of the leftover beef from lunch – when I found myself standing at the foot of the attic stairs. I may have decided to go to the kitchen, but my feet had other ideas. As I stood at the bottom of the attic stairs, the muffled creak of an opening door in another part of the house sent me scurrying up the stairs and closing the attic door softly behind me. The moon's light was reflecting off the Blue Room's mirror, although the light didn't extend to the shadowed corners of the room.

As I passed the mirror I saw something flit across its cracked corner, but when I checked behind me there was nothing there.

"Idiot," I said aloud, but my voice was unsteady and I couldn't shake the feeling that I was being watched.

I paused again in front of the hinged chest and tried to lift its lid, but a rusted padlock held it firmly in place. I shook the padlock from side to side, but it held fast, and I soon gave up trying.

At the octagonal window I caught sight of the sea beyond the bluff's edge. The moonlight traced a silver path across the dark water. The scene in the front garden was shades of grey. Down below, leading away from Vinegar House, was the lighter grey of the driveway. To my left was the tree house. Further down were the trees that lined the driveway. And something else … there was something in the shadows that had shadows of their own …

Before I had a chance to think further there was a rustling above my head that made my scalp crawl. Visions of bats or mice or … what other things rustled like that in the dead of night? I shone my phone light into the rafters, but the beam skipped about as my hand shook. It was too feeble to be any use anyway. The groan of the attic door opening made me jump with fright, and a sudden voice from the darkness said, "I nearly locked you in."

It was Mrs Skelton. She was wearing a long flannel nightgown buttoned up to her collarbone. Her usual wispy hair hung in a skinny braid that fell over one shoulder. She flinched as I turned my light onto her face.

"Sorry," I said, moving the light.

I could see she was waiting on an explanation – a reason that I might be poking about in the attic in the dead of night.

"I was hungry …"

"Yes?"

I watched her step towards the locked trunk and rest a hand on its lid.

"A strange time of day to be getting hungry, if you ask me," she said.

"I saw the light. From the attic …" I trailed off and listened to the crash of the waves in the distance.

"Which is why I'm here. I remembered I'd left the door open this evening," said Mrs Skelton smoothly. "Though I don't remember leaving a light on."

"Moonlight," I said. I wondered why she had been in the attic at all.

"Ah."

We stood, silent for a moment.

"Well," I said.

She stood aside, and I scuttled down the stairs, my mobile torch beam bobbing in crazy arcs over the staircase and hallway. I heard the firm whump as the attic door shut and the definite click of the lock as it moved into place. I had just reached my bedroom door when she called out softly, "Not hungry any more?"

"No," I said. Then added, "I'll wait for breakfast."

I fell into my room, closed the door and leaned against it, waiting for my heart to stop knocking against my ribs. There were three things I knew for sure in that moment:

1. I was too old to be scared of someone like Mrs Skelton.

2. There were secrets in the locked trunk, and I was going to discover what they were.

3. I had seen grey shadows near the tree house and I was pretty sure I knew who they were.

I pulled the unread note from the dresser and read it by the light of my mobile.

Dear R,
I waited for you last night. Why didn't you come?
I'll be waiting there again tonight.
Let's sort this out.
L

I put the note away and hopped into bed. I listened to the sounds of the house as it breathed in the night and the shudder of the plumbing as if water had been turned off. Then I realised that had been the noise which had pulled me from sleep at 2.47 am. The sound of the plumbing.

It could have been anything – someone getting a

glass of water, or flushing a toilet. Or just a tap not turned off all the way. Yet I couldn't shake the memory of the empty bathroom with its fogged mirror and water splashing into the tub.

My hot water bottle was lukewarm, but I held onto it tightly to stop my body shivering. And I waited for sleep to come.

Chapter 20

That holiday at Vinegar House, I discovered something about myself that I wasn't proud of – if I wasn't supposed to have something, then that's the very thing I desperately wanted to have. There were two things out of bounds for me during that time. The first thing was the attic. The second was Luke Hart.

I thought about Luke night and day.

Day and night.

I imagined that he'd never met Rumer. That I was the one he'd spent the lazy hot days at Ocean Side with.

I invented clever conversations where I had just the right answer. Dreamed of us dancing closely. Amazing dances where we both knew all the steps.

I daydreamed how it would feel to hold his hand again.

To stroll along the beach leaning into his warmth.

I wanted to make him laugh.

I
wanted
Luke
Hart.

Rumer spent more time out of her room than before, but there were hours when the door was shut and nothing could budge her. Not even Mrs Skelton's infamous banana muffins. (In fact, I shut *myself* in my room when *they* were on offer.) Even when she was out of her room, we didn't have much to say to each other. Rumer was distracted, and I didn't want to talk about it. Didn't want her confiding her love-life to me.

I tried to fill my days as much as I could. I couldn't rely on texting. The mobile phone signal dropped out often – so much to the point that it was out more than it was in. Besides, there was hardly anyone to text. As usual, I'd hidden when things got too tough and now I was in no-man's-land without a friend.

My day kind of went like this:

1. Up for breakfast every morning.

2. I'd clear the dishes. (Although I don't know why I bothered because I never got it right. If I stacked them on the sink, Mrs Skelton moved them to the

pine kitchen table. If I left them on the table, that's the very place she needed to be doing something else. The woman drove me mad.)

3. Check the attic door. (Which was always locked.)

4. Then I'd go for a walk down to the beach to see if anything interesting had washed up on the sand overnight. (I'd gone back to collecting sea glass. I guess some things never change. Sometimes Rumer came with me, but usually she skipped breakfast and didn't get up until much later.)

5. Back to the library for some homework. (I'd found that the desk in the library caught the morning sun. Once Mrs Skelton worked out my routine, she organised for Mr Chilvers to have a small fire burning in the fireplace by the time I arrived each morning. On the face of it, this was an unexpected kindness on behalf of the housekeeper. Of course I knew the real reason behind the kindness – this just added another chore to Mr Chilvers's day and that would have made her happy.)

6. A cooked lunch. (Usually I was still full from breakfast.)

7. After lunch I'd try and do a chore for Mrs Skelton so I could cross that off my list for when the Colonel rang. (He was sounding quite cheery on the phone,

which was making me cross. He and Mum had been doing some day trips – sightseeing around the place – and catching up with some of Mum's old friends. Nice work for some.)

8. Next, check the attic door.

9. In the afternoon I'd take another walk to the beach. Or sometimes I'd walk up past the stables or climb up to the tree house or go through the photo albums in the library.

Grandma tried to teach Rumer and me how to play a card game called five hundred, but Rumer couldn't get the hang of bowers. Also it meant we needed Mrs Skelton as a fourth player, and she would grumble so much about not getting her work done, that we'd switch to a simpler game like Hearts or Up and Down the River. Playing any kind of game with Grandma was not fun. She always liked to dissect where a particular player went wrong or how something could have been done better. It was like playing games with the Colonel, and I now had an insight into what it must have been like for him growing up. Grandma and Rumer both liked to win, which didn't leave a lot of space for me.

I only allowed myself two peeks of Luke Hart per day. If I was having a particularly boring time, I'd allow myself an extra peek just to get through the day. Sometimes I'd watch him go about his work as I sat perched in the tree house. Sometimes I'd see him from my bedroom window – bent over at the waist, steam rising from him in the cold air as he worked the garden beds that lined the driveway – or through the kitchen window, chopping kindling, as I was stacking dishes.

Then one morning he was in the library. I stumbled into the room on Tuesday morning, my arms filled with books and papers, to find Luke setting a fire in the grate.

"Hello," he said. "Just getting this going for you."

"Oh." I tried to recall one of my incredibly clever conversations I'd been working on. "Thanks," was all I could muster.

I dumped everything onto the desk and twitched back the curtains to let in more light. I fussed about, setting out my books, notebook and pens. Then I said, "So how's the job going?"

"Good. Busy."

"Well ... that's good." I rearranged my pens.

One of Grandma's cats swished into the room, jumped up onto the desk, and promptly sat on my notebook.

"How's your grandmother?"

"Nanna," I said automatically. "Good. Good, thank you."

"So how are you going?" he asked. I watched him light a match and hold it against a balled up newspaper page. "Must be a bit boring?"

"It's okay." I pointed to my books. "Getting my homework done."

Hmmm, good one Freya, I thought, nothing like stating the obvious.

"Probably good that you're not at Homsea right now anyway," he said.

I watched the flame from the paper lick at the dry twigs and kindling. I shifted in my seat. I could hear the cat purring. "What?"

"You know." He seemed uncomfortable. There was a crackle as a twig caught alight.

"What?" I wanted to open the window. I needed air. All of a sudden the room was warm enough.

"That whole thing. With that Suzette girl. Probably good to let it all … you know … die down."

"How …?"

"Facebook," he said. "Haven't been online since I've been here. Probably yesterday's news by now."

Luke Hart, the one person I'd been thinking of day and night, knew that I had been accused of kissing another girl's boyfriend. There was a photo of it on Facebook. This was the big issue that I'd been avoiding. The whole reason I was happy to be staying away from Facebook. It's not what it looked like, but that didn't matter. Hamish Thomson, Suzette Crompt's boyfriend, had kissed me as a dare at Tara Wilcock's birthday party, and someone had taken a photo. Life was so boring at Homsea High that there was nothing else going on. The whole thing had blown way out of proportion.

And Luke knew all about it.

By now the fire was burning brightly. Luke added some larger pieces of wood and brushed the bark from his hands. I was so embarrassed I couldn't look at him.

"Hamish is a nice guy," said Luke. "I've played footy with him—"

Luke thought I was actually interested in Hamish Thomson?

"No ..." Did I really want him to think that I was that sort of girl? The sort of girl that kissed her friend's boyfriend? A Rumer sort of girl? But did I really want to tell him the truth – that I was stupid enough to be at the wrong end of someone's ten-dollar bet?

"Thanks for the fire," I said, and I turned back to my books as if I couldn't waste another minute away from them.

The cat was looking up at me like I was a big liar – which I was.

Chapter 21

Wednesday arrived with a bright shining sun, no wind in sight and another note. For a winter's day it was positively hot. This time there was no envelope under Rumer's door, just a piece of paper folded over twice, and the letter R in that same square writing on the outside of the note.

R

These are the things I love about you.

Your smile, which starts at the corners and works its way towards your cheeks.

Your hands, which float in the air whenever you talk.

Your hair when it brushes my cheek.

Meet me at 12.

L

I tucked the note into my dresser drawer and practised my own smile in front of the mirror. One of Grandma's cats, Cinnamon, watched with interest from the end of my bed.

"Oh, you wrote this note for me? How sweet!" I moved my hands about as I spoke, but just looked like I was being attacked by a plague of flies. I gave up trying to be like Rumer.

The only thing I found on my early morning walk to the beach was a slightly battered styrofoam surfboard with a big chunk out of one end. It made me think of the movie *Jaws,* and I shuddered a little as I threw it up onto the rocks near the track – planning to take it back with me when I left. The sand looked so soft and inviting that I lay down and let the sun's warmth soak into my bones.

I was trying to work out how I would open the lock of the attic trunk. Maybe bolt cutters or a key. One of the keys hanging from Mrs Skelton's neck would probably do the trick. I wondered if she ever took the keys off, or if she slept with them – even showered with them. I wouldn't put it past her.

How to get those keys?

I wished I could talk to Luke about my problem. He'd have a good idea.

I felt myself slipping into that place that isn't quite awake and isn't quite asleep, when a shadow fell over

179

me and I looked up to see Luke. He was standing watching me, his work cap pulled low over his forehead. I couldn't see his face properly. My heart set up a clumsy gallop.

"You *are* down here!" he said.

"Yep," I said. I closed my eyes against the sun's glare and felt the sand shift next to me as Luke sat down.

"Your grandmother's after you," he said. "Something about peeling potatoes or something."

"Wonder what her last slave died of," I said.

He laughed.

It wasn't that funny.

"Why didn't she send Rumer down to get me? Actually, why doesn't Rumer do the potatoes?" I threw my cousin's name into the air twice – a challenge that Luke ignored.

What I really wanted to say was, "How can you be interested in someone like Rumer after she was so mean to you?"

What I really wanted to say was, "How can you not be interested in me?"

But sometimes it's hard to say what you really want to.

"Dunno," he said. Then he laughed again. "Do you remember when you swam out to Seal Rock?"

I opened my eyes to see him looking out over the waves.

"I wasn't trying to swim to Seal Rock." I sat up and leaned on one elbow. "I was just … It doesn't matter." I shaded my eyes and looked out to the rock, which was covered in seagulls.

"What doesn't matter?" he asked.

I lay back and shut my eyes. "I can't remember."

My head hoped Luke would go away.

My heartbeat quickened and hoped he would stay.

I cranked one eyelid open and watched him lie down on the sand. He was so close our shoulders were touching.

"Do you remember that holiday at Ocean Side?" He shifted a little closer. I could feel the heat of his shoulder branding mine. "The one where it rained for two weeks solid?"

"Hmm, mmm," I said. The sun was beating down nicely and making me feel drowsy. I wished I could forget about Rumer and Luke. Luke and Rumer. Together again.

"Your dad taught us how to play canasta," he said.

"Ruleman," I said.

"Remember how the parents kept pretending to lose so we'd keep playing?"

"Not the Colonel," I said. "'Winning isn't everything, Freya, but losing is nothing'."

"He does hate to lose," said Luke. "Remember that Easter? We went camping and lost all our chocolate eggs? Rosie ate them—"

"Silver paper and all."

"I was sure your dad was going to shove his hand down her throat to get them back."

"I loved that dog." I giggled.

"Yup. Do you still collect sea glass?" he asked.

"No. I don't do that any more," I said, thinking about the nice collection I had lined up on my dresser.

The dresser. The notes …

I shifted slightly away from him.

"Oh, I'm playing in the Firsts football team this year."

"I know." I didn't want Luke to think I was stalking him. "I heard. I think Isabella told me."

"How's your *Nanna*?"

I noticed that he'd gotten her name right and I smiled. "Much better. Thank you."

"When are your parents coming home?" he asked.

"Not sure. Next week sometime, I think."

I didn't want to think about going home. I just wanted to be where I was forever, lying on the beach next to Luke, talking like we used to before everything got messed up.

"I haven't seen you at the jetty. It's been ages."

It had been exactly twenty months since I'd stopped trotting down to the jetty on a Saturday morning like a faithful lapdog, waiting for Luke Hart to appear, swinging his bucket and giving me a wave. Nearly two years since he'd first set eyes on Rumer at Ocean Side and fallen under her spell. Basically, a whole lifetime since she'd dumped him like a piece of rubbish. She hadn't even bothered to find a bin. And yet, he seemed to have forgotten all that.

But I hadn't.

The thought slid from my mind as I said, "I've been busy."

I felt him shift beside me a little and heard him sigh. I tried not to think about what that sigh might mean. I matched my breathing to the rhythm of the waves breaking on the shore. The sun was making the inside of my eyelids a pulsing red. I felt my body sink further into the sand as my muscles relaxed and my fingers unfurled from their tight fists.

"Have you ever taken the dinghy out?" he asked.

"The what?"

"The dinghy. The little boat over near the rocks."

"Oh. No. That's ancient," I said.

"Pity," said Luke. "I reckon there'd be fish out there."

"Hmmmm."

"I saw some hand reels in the stables."

"Hmmmm."

"How's the play rehearsal going?"

"Yeah, good." I'd worry about that lie later.

"I think it's great you're doing the play."

I squirmed a little.

"You have something …" he said.

"Hmmmm?"

The light behind my closed eyelids darkened, and I looked up to see Luke leaning over me.

This is what I'd been waiting for since I first saw him working in the garden at Vinegar House.

Strike that.

This is what I'd been waiting for since forever.

I could feel his breath on my face. I smelled his Luke Hart smell that I knew so well. I was drowning in his eyes. If he leaned in a little closer our lips would surely meet like magnets attracted to each other.

"You have …" he grazed my cheek with his fingers and held up a small piece of dried seaweed, "… this on your cheek."

Then I gasped as someone said, "Oh, *there* you are."

It was Rumer. My cheeks burned.

Luke rose slowly from the sand and brushed it from him. "You're up early," he said to Rumer as if they shared a private joke, and I watched her blush.

I wanted to tell them that I knew. Knew they'd been meeting in the dead of night. But my tongue couldn't find the words. I felt my Luke Hart slipping away, replaced by the stupid Luke Hart who wrote love notes to my stupid cousin.

"Back to it, I guess," he said with a smile.

Rumer and I both watched as Luke sauntered up the bluff path then disappeared behind the tea-tree.

"Well, well," said Rumer. She gave me a piercing look, then turned on her heel and followed him.

And I felt a small thrill of victory, though I hadn't won anything at all.

Chapter 22

Mum was sounding happier each time she rang. I knew I should have been happy too, the way things had worked out. I mean … Nanna was better, Isabella was still on holidays, Oscar hadn't broken anything, Holly was busy being French, Luke and Rumer were meeting up in the dead of night and everyone was happy, right? Meanwhile, I was stuck at Vinegar House while even Grandma was set to leave the house on her big trip to Port Eden. You'd think she was going on a six-month holiday the amount of fuss that she and Mrs Skelton carried on with.

On Thursday morning I woke early to the sound of banging and thumping down the hallway. I poked my head out to see Mrs Skelton lugging two suitcases down the attic staircase.

"Can I help?" I asked.

"No, no, it's very early," said Mrs Skelton. "You just stay in your nice warm bed. I'll be fine."

I was getting to understand Mrs Skelton's language. This meant, "If you don't want to end up with burnt toast, you'd better help me right now".

I helped Mrs Skelton who grumbled all the way down the hallway. "Too much luggage for one person, if you ask me," I heard her say.

We left the empty suitcases at Grandma's bedroom door, and I went back to my room and chose my clothes for the day.

My hands were freezing and I tried to warm them on the coil heater. When I looked out the window I could see Luke was already up and about. He was pushing the rusted wheelbarrow down the driveway, a hat pulled down around his ears.

I didn't want to think about Luke any more.

I couldn't help but think about him.

Night and day.

The air in my bedroom was so cold that my warm breath was fogging the window. I had a sudden urge to go to the attic, but when I checked, the door was locked as usual.

Rumer turned up for breakfast as if to make sure that Grandma was really leaving. After breakfast there was a lot of ordering about from Grandma and running up and down the stairs for last minute things.

Finally we were standing in the entry hall waiting for last-minute instructions.

"I need my wrap," Grandma called out to Mrs Skelton who was snapping suitcase locks at the top of the stairs. I heard the housekeeper grumbling as she left the case in search of the wrap.

Two overnight cases and a large tapestry beauty case already stood at the front door. I was itching to look inside the beauty case, wondering if it was Mrs Skelton's or Grandma Vinegar's. I couldn't imagine either woman needing so many beauty products.

Grandma seemed on edge and distracted.

"I have left a list near the entry hall telephone," she said, pointing to the phone as if Rumer and I were six-year-olds. "You will find the phone number and address of our motel there, as well as our neighbour's number, Mr Craddock. In case of emergency."

The Craddocks lived twenty kilometres as the crow flew, and though they were technically our neighbours, I didn't see that they'd be much use in the case of an emergency.

"We'll be fine, Grandma," said Rumer, impatiently.

Another snap of the locks from upstairs announced Mrs Skelton was back.

"Did you get the paisley wrap, Livinia? I think that's

best for keeping out the chills of Port Eden," said Grandma as she unzipped then rezipped the case at her feet.

I wondered who Grandma was talking to then realised she meant Mrs Skelton.

Mrs Skelton unbent from her task.

"Paisley wrap?" she repeated.

"Yes, the paisley," said Grandma. "Now don't forget to feed the cats," she continued, looking at me. "A little treat tonight and main meal tomorrow morning. And don't let them go wandering around outside after dark. I've put their cushions in the corner of the kitchen."

"A wrap's a wrap, if you ask me," I heard the housekeeper mutter as she took a lilac-coloured wrap from the case and marched off in the direction of Grandma's room.

A car horn sounded from the driveway.

"There's Mr Chilvers now," said Grandma, as if he'd driven hours to get here, instead of just getting the car out of the ancient garage.

She fussed about, trying to pull up the retractable handle on the case until Rumer grabbed the case from Grandma and pulled the handle up in one swift motion.

"I don't know what was wrong with the old suitcase

design," said Grandma, looking at Rumer's black nail polish. "Feel free to use anything you need in the guest bathroom, girls. Sunscreen. Moisturiser. Nail polish remover …"

"All good, thanks, Gran," said Rumer, gruffly.

"Yes, well, that really isn't correct grammar–"

The car horn sounded again.

"Oh, Mr Chilvers … Livinia!" called out Grandma.

Mrs Skelton appeared at the top of the stairs. "I can't find your paisley, Mrs Kramer. Where do you think you've put it?"

Grandma waved a hand in the air. "There's no time to look now, Livinia. Just get the lilac one. That will have to do."

Mrs Skelton looked like she might tell Grandma what she could do with her lilac shawl.

"Lilac," repeated Mrs Skelton. "What a good idea." And again she disappeared.

"So you have the phone numbers, girls," repeated Grandma. "Mrs Skelton and I shall be back by tomorrow afternoon. Mr Chilvers has some family business to attend to in Port Eden so he won't be back until much later this afternoon. And then of course he will be leaving before tomorrow lunchtime to pick us up. You can always ring him at the cottage if you need

190

anything tonight. The number's near the phone. Mrs Skelton has left dinner in the refrigerator for the four of you. You just need to heat it up."

I wondered who "the four of you were", then realised that she meant Mr Chilvers and Luke.

"We'll be fine, Grandma," said Rumer with a yawn.

"I have my regular medical check-up and my eye specialist tomorrow morning and then a meeting with my solicitor, Mr Lipshut," continued Grandma Vinegar.

Rumer's giggle turned into a cough when Grandma looked at her crossly.

"And, of course, Mrs Skelton will be making sure I get to all my appointments on time." She paused, looking at us closely, eyes narrowed. "Perhaps it's best if you don't have a fire in the television room tonight. Remember to turn the wall heating down when you go to bed–"

"Yes, Grandma," I said, thinking I might not only leave it on but turn it up full bore.

"Make sure Luke stops for lunch today. Mrs Skelton has made his lunch, but he'll also need a hot drink. The wind is going to turn. I can feel it in my bones."

"Lunch," I said. There was no way I was taking Luke his lunch. Rumer could get it for him. There'd be no need to pretend everything was fine any more, now that Grandma was leaving.

"If the power goes out, you'll find candles in the top drawer next to the wood stove in the kitchen. You'll find the matches there too."

"Matches," I repeated, nodding.

"There are also some torches in the library. You'll find fresh batteries there as well."

"Batteries." I nodded again.

"Sometimes the water heater flame goes out. If you leave the laundry door open that can happen. Wait until Mr Chilvers comes back. He knows how to start it up again. It's very cantankerous. I don't want you girls touching it."

"Right."

"If Fay Anthony rings about the fundraiser, you can tell her I'm not contributing a cent until I know how my money's being spent. Last year's money was spent on a coffee machine at the Port Eden Youth Centre. What are they drinking coffee for? Water's the best thing for a growing body. Not what I'd call charity."

"Uh-huh." I could see Rumer picking away at the polish on her fingernails.

"Charity begins at home, after all," Grandma said, though this didn't seem to make sense to me. "I must get Mr Chilvers onto that wall crack before it gets much bigger. Where is that woman?" she said, looking up the stairs.

Grandma picked up the phone and listened for a dial tone as if to make sure it was still working. Rumer yawned loudly.

"Make sure you go outside sometime today and get some air," said Grandma. "You both spend far too much time hunched over your books. You'll end up with bad posture and back braces."

Rumer and I both nodded. I noticed my cousin stood a little straighter and pulled her shoulders back.

"Livinia!" Grandma called out sternly, then she turned back to us. "Now don't think I don't know that you'll turn on the television as soon as I leave. But if it's on for too long it gets overheated and shuts down. Then you have to leave it off for the rest of the day. Just remember that."

"Gotcha," I said.

Grandma frowned. "Maybe you should come with us …"

The *thump, thump, thump* of a case coming down the stairs distracted Grandma from her train of thought. I rushed upstairs to help Mrs Skelton who seemed to be enjoying the noise she was making. Rumer opened the front door and asked Mr Chilvers to help with the luggage, as if she were at the Hilton instead of Vinegar House. Mr Chilvers, not in his work overalls today, hitched up his pants as if unused to such foreign clothes and opened the car boot.

Grandma's car was an old model Mercedes that reminded me of a luxury liner. Mr Chilvers's breath rose in clouds about his face in the crisp air as he loaded the luggage into the car boot. Mrs Skelton twisted a long tartan scarf about her neck, then settled herself primly into the back seat. Grandma frowned up at the sky.

"The weather forecaster predicted a sunny day with light winds," she said, "but I think there's a thunderstorm coming."

I looked up at the sky. It was blue and decorated with only a few fluffy white clouds.

"I saw a line of ants in the kitchen this morning. A sure sign of rain," said Grandma.

"See ya, Grandma," said Rumer, pointedly.

Grandma Vinegar was still pondering the possibility of a thunderstorm as she sat in the front passenger seat and Mr Chilvers shut her door.

Rumer and I stood in the driveway, waiting for the car to pull out.

"I think she's losing it," said Rumer, giving a little wave.

The front passenger door window rolled down as the engine purred into life.

"Lock the doors," said Grandma. She looked me straight in the eye. "Be careful."

The last thing I saw as the car drove away was Grandma adjusting a colourful paisley shawl about her shoulders.

Rumer went straight to the TV room, but I had other plans. I was certain that Mrs Skelton would have left her set of keys hanging from one of the key hooks in the kitchen, but when I checked they weren't there.

"Old bag," I said, kicking the cupboard door.

Mrs Skelton had obviously taken the keys with her.

Still, there were other ways to get into a locked room. There were plenty of tools in the stables. There was bound to be something there that could open the attic door and the locked trunk.

I'd show her.

Chapter 23

Sometimes I think I'm a masochist. I'm always the one to partner Dad at cards, even though he's never happy with the cards I play. I'm always the one who washes the dog, even though I know I'll be wearing dog shampoo by the end of it all. And I'm always the one who goes looking for Rumer, even though I know she's just going to be rude and obnoxious to me.

Before I left for the stables to look for boltcutters, I checked in with Rumer in the TV room. She was watching some loud morning show, her feet propped up on the coffee table in front of her. Grandma Vinegar would have had a fit. I was surprised Luke wasn't at her side already.

"I'm just going out for a walk," I said, standing in the doorway.

"Suit yourself," said Rumer, barely taking her eyes from the screen. She waved her mobile phone about wildly for a second and said flatly, "No signal! Typical."

There was a weird moment when I wanted to confess about the notes, and I might have, except Rumer said sharply, "I can't wait to get out of here. This place is a hole. The only good thing about this holiday has been getting my homework done."

It seemed Rumer wasn't going to own up to what she and Luke had been up to.

"It's not that bad," I said.

"I guess it depends on what you're used to," Rumer said with a yawn. "I don't suppose it's much different from Homsea."

"What do you mean?" I asked.

"You know. Small town. Nothing much to do. You'd be used to it." She flicked to another channel with the remote control.

I was sick of Rumer and her put-down ways.

"Although I heard you'd stirred things up a bit before the holidays," Rumer said with a lazy smile. "Kissing someone else's boyfriend? Didn't think you had it in you, cuz."

I was sick of her taking things that weren't hers to take.

"Dad said that he might get back early from the conference, depends if he can get a flight," said Rumer.

"I told him he owed me big time. I wish the twins were here. They're always fun."

She flicked to another channel.

"At least the old bat's gone. She was seriously driving me crazy."

Flick.

"And that gardener gives me the creeps. What's his problem? I asked him to do something for me the other day and he said Grandma paid him, not me. And then he said she barely paid him enough as it was, without him having to do extra work. I think I might tell Grandma when they get back. Serves him right if she fires him on the spot."

I was sick of the world where there were two sets of rules – one rule for Rumer and another for everyone else.

"Are you coming in or what?" she asked.

I shook my head.

"Well, shut the door, will you? I'm trying to keep warm here," she said.

"You shut it," I said.

And I left her with her mouth wide open …

But of course, that's not what really happened.

"Are you coming in or what?" she asked.

I shook my head.

"Well, shut the door, will you? I'm trying to keep warm here," she said.

So I shut the door quietly behind me.

❋ ❋ ❋

There was nothing in the stables that looked like it might open an attic door or a locked chest. If Mr Chilvers had a toolbox, it wasn't there. I thought about asking Luke, but I couldn't face him.

When I checked my mobile, the no signal sign flashed at me. I suddenly wanted to be home. I wanted to be walking down the main street of Homsea where everyone knew me and at least half of them would stop and say hello if I looked like I needed company.

I wanted to sit in Miss Maudy's Quilt Barn and hear her talk about the amazing travels she'd had when she was younger.

I wanted to wave to Rudy Heinrich pointing his radar gun out of his parked police car, or drop a flower off at the war memorial, or check out the latest specials on Porky Sudholz's blackboard.

But most of all I wanted to be sitting at the end of the jetty, feet dangling over the side, waiting for some sucker squid to take the bait as I shot the breeze with the Luke Hart that I used to know.

But that was never going to happen again.

So I guess I *was* small town. And though Rumer meant it as a put-down, I kind of liked the idea.

As I walked back to the house I noticed the clouds were slowly blocking out the blue of the sky. The breeze from the bluff had lifted and it whistled around my ears. There was no way I could go back to the TV room. I thought I might study in the library for a while.

I tried not to think about the love notes hidden away in my dresser drawer. By the time I set myself up in the library it was already eleven o'clock. I decided to make myself a hot drink before I settled into it. When I returned to the desk, a fire was crackling into life in the fireplace. Luke had obviously been and gone.

I was happy I missed him.

I hoped he would come back.

After half an hour of history, I snapped my textbook shut in disgust. I couldn't concentrate. Outside, the wind had picked up, snapping the trees back and forth like floggers at a football match. I looked around at the family portraits on the walls. I put another log of wood on the fire, then pulled out the family photo albums and flicked through them. By the third album it dawned on me what I was doing. I was looking for photos of Rumer's mother. A happy family snap of Rumer and her mum and dad. A tender mother and child moment caught for the camera. But there was nothing. The only photos of Rumer as an infant were either by herself, or with her dad, cousins or Grandma Vinegar. I hurried through the rest of the albums, then started again, but there was nothing. All the albums I'd looked at only started with the birth of the first grandchild, Julia. There must have been older albums around.

I scoured the library shelves again. On the second look through, I spotted something slightly hidden between two medical dictionaries. If I'd been doing my dusting properly, I would have found it days before. It was a cracked leather-bound album, and as I pulled it out a photo of Rumer slid to the floor. She was wearing a striped top that I had never seen on her before, and the colour of the photo was faded. Then I realised that I wasn't looking at Rumer at all. This was an old photo. It had to be Rumer's mother. I wondered why she'd been hidden away.

"What have you got there?" Rumer was standing at the door.

I shoved the photo back into the album.

"Just the old photos," I said.

The phone in the hallway jangled loudly. Rumer shrugged and answered it, while I slipped out the photo and stuck it in my pocket.

I heard her speak a few words. By the time I reached the hallway, she'd hung up.

"Who was that?" I asked.

"Wrong number," she said, not looking at me. "Did they leave us lunch or what?"

And she went to the kitchen without waiting for an answer.

The phone rang again, and I picked it up quickly.

"Hello? Hello? This line isn't working, Livinia. There's no one there." It was Grandma.

"Hello, Grandma," I said loudly into the phone.

"Ah, Freya? Is that you, Freya?"

"Yes, Grandma."

"Good. Now listen to me, we have reached Port Eden. Is everything all right there?"

"Yes, Grandma."

"Good. Now Mr Chilvers has some business in town, but he will be home late this afternoon."

She had already told us that.

"Okay," I said.

"Is everything all right there?" she asked.

"Everything's fine, Grandma."

"All right."

I could hear heavy breathing from her end of the phone.

"You will ring my contact number if you need anything, Freya?" she said, eventually.

"We're fine, Grandma," I said.

"Yes, yes, Livinia." She said away from the phone. "I have to go now, Freya, this is costing me a fortune."

Then Grandma Vinegar hung up before I had a chance to say goodbye.

Rumer emerged from the kitchen with a large sandwich.

"I didn't make you anything," she said with her mouth half-filled with food. "I didn't know what you wanted."

As she sauntered off to the TV room, I felt the edge of the photo poking out from my pocket.

And I left it there.

Chapter 24

I took the old photo album upstairs to my bedroom and spent the next few hours looking through it. I'd always thought of Rumer's dad as a Kramer family member because he looked so much like the rest of us – brown hair, solid build. But of course, Rumer's surname was Grey. Rumer Grey. Which meant that it was her mother who had belonged to the Kramer family tree. That's why there were so many photos of her mother's younger years in the old family album. But that still didn't solve the mystery of why there were no photos of Rumer with her mother. And why the family never talked about Rumer's mother. I pulled the photo from my pocket and studied the inscription on the back.

Bec, Form 5.

Even with the faded colours, the resemblance to Rumer was uncanny. I wondered how my aunty had died.

There was still no phone reception so I couldn't text Isabella. As I wandered downstairs for a late lunch I realised I hadn't given Luke his midday meal. I shoved some wood into the wood stove, then pulled the plated up meal from the warmer where Mrs Skelton had placed it many hours before.

"Is that mine?"

Luke stood at the door knocking the soil from his shoes.

"Sorry. Yes. I forgot. Come in." I placed the plate on the kitchen table, grabbed some cutlery and a glass. "Do you want a drink?" I asked.

"Just water will do," he said, washing his hands in the sink.

"You can eat in the dining room if you like," I offered.

"I usually eat at the cottage," Luke explained. "Here's okay."

He sat down to eat when the phone rang. I heard Rumer pick up, then moments later she came into the kitchen.

"Oh, hello," she said to Luke, coolly. "How's work going?"

"Enough of it," he said. "How's everything going?"

Luke seemed to be putting a lot of emphasis on the

word "everything" and I wanted to say "I know what you are talking about", but of course I didn't.

"*Everything* is fine," said Rumer.

"Who was on the phone?" I asked.

"Nobody," said Rumer. "At least, nobody who wanted to talk. I thought I heard breathing, but they hung up."

A gust of wind rattled the kitchen window.

"Do you think it was Grandma?" I asked.

Rumer shrugged. She opened the fridge door, wrinkled her nose, then closed it again. "I'm going out for a walk," she said. "Down to the beach."

There was a message there for someone to follow her, and I knew it wasn't me.

"Okay," I said.

"I'll be back in time for dinner," she said.

"Dinner?" I asked.

"I should be starving by then."

I felt Luke's eyes on me.

"And I've got a load of washing on," she continued, "so can you just chuck those clothes in the dryer when they're ready? But not my blue top. That can just go in the drying room."

She was nearly out the door before I managed to say something that had taken me a lifetime to say.

"No."

"See ya, Luke," she said, as if she hadn't heard me.

"I said no!"

Rumer turned around and looked at me, one hand on her hip.

"Okay, well, just leave the blue top out and–"

I shook my head.

"Oh, Freya. What is your problem?"

"I know what's going on," I said.

Her hand left her hip. "What ..."

Luke scraped his chair back.

"Stay!" I said.

"You're mad," said Rumer as she turned towards the door.

"I know about the notes," I said.

She stopped but didn't face me.

"I know what's going on so we can all stop pretending," I said. "And no, Rumer. I am not making dinner. I am not doing your laundry. And I'm not putting up with you any longer ..."

Of course, that's not quite what happened.

"I'm going out for a walk," Rumer said. "Down to the beach."

There was a message there for someone to follow her, and I knew it wasn't me.

"Okay," I said.

"I'll be back in time for dinner," she said.

"Dinner?" I asked.

"I should be starving by then."

I felt Luke's eyes on me.

"And I've got a load of washing on," she continued, "so can you just chuck those clothes in the dryer when they're ready? But not my blue top. That can just go in the drying room."

She was nearly out the door before I managed to say something that had taken me a lifetime to say.

"No."

"See ya, Luke," she said, as if she hadn't heard me.

"I said no, Rumer!"

Rumer turned around and looked at me, one hand on her hip.

Then I walked out of the kitchen and slammed the door behind me.

❋ ❋ ❋

An hour later the phone jangled in the hall and I had to rush downstairs to pick it up.

"No one's answering, Livinia," I hear Grandma Vinegar say.

"Hello? Grandma?"

"Freya? Is that you, Freya?"

"Yes, Grandma. Did you ring just before?" I asked.

"Now listen, Freya. Something's happened and I'm afraid Mr Chilvers won't be–"

I didn't get to hear what Mr Chilvers wouldn't be doing because the line went dead. I jiggled the phone and tried to dial out, but there was just the faintest ghost of a whistle on the line, so I gave up. I checked my mobile and still had no signal, then jumped a little as a gust of wind rattled the front door.

Thinking Grandma's weather forecast might be spot on, I fed more wood into the wood stove and into the fireplace in the library, just in case the power failed and we ended up with no heating. Armed with a candle and a box of matches, I went to the TV room and watched a couple of hours of very boring afternoon TV. It was so boring, I fell asleep on the couch and only woke up when the television made a loud noise and the screen image disappeared. The power was down.

It was late in the afternoon judging by the grey light outside. The wind was slamming against the house and an upstairs door shut with a loud bang. Rumer had obviously returned from her walk when I was asleep. From the kitchen I peered down the back garden for a sign of Mr Chilvers, but I couldn't see the garage and couldn't be bothered going outside to check. Maybe Mr Chilvers had been delayed? Maybe that was Grandma's message. There was no sign of smoke from the cottage, and I wondered where Luke was working. I silently thanked Mrs Skelton for her wood stove, as I cooked up a jar of spaghetti sauce and a slab of minced meat. Then I checked the fridge and added grated carrot to help make it more interesting. A couple of times I heard the creak of footsteps from upstairs and once I heard a noise that sounded like furniture being moved about. I wondered what my cousin was up to.

Okay, you're going to think I'm crazy at this point, but I'm going to tell you what happened next and you're not going to believe it. Which will make two of us.

One moment I was in the kitchen, and the next I was standing on the front door steps looking out to Seal Rock. It's like something made me do it. And from where I stood I could see what could have been a very large seabird or a small boat bobbing up and down on the waves. I stood there for a full minute but the thing just stayed where it was, bobbing up and down. I went back inside to the kitchen, stirred the spaghetti sauce then put the saucepan lid on tightly. Back on the front steps I could see the boat/bird was still bobbing about in the water. Every pore in my body was telling me there was something wrong. I had an argument with myself – it was getting too late to go for a walk down to Bluff Beach – but it was a short argument, and I wasn't winning.

I grabbed a torch from the library and a coat from my bedroom. For a moment I was tempted to get Rumer to come with me, but when she didn't answer the knock on her door I left without her. I took the short cut down to Bluff Beach and the tea-tree rattled in the wind that gusted every now and then. A low distant rumble announced a coming storm and I was already wishing myself back in the warm kitchen of Vinegar House. When I got down to the beach there were no surprises. The old dinghy had gone, which is what I'd feared. Only the rope remained, coiled up like a giant snake, one end still tethered in the sand. Out near Seal Rock, the upturned dinghy bobbed up and down on the waves. The gulls were squabbling nearby, then I realised that I could hear another noise.

"Freya! Freya!"

The boat had swung around a little and now I could see someone hanging onto its side. Someone in a red windcheater.

"Freya!"

Rumer is my least favourite cousin. Have I told you that? Even so, I couldn't leave her to drown at Seal Rock. But I didn't know what to do. I was too scared to go to the house for Luke, just in case Rumer was gone by the time I returned.

I stamped my foot. "Rumer!"

I looked around for help. There was no way I could throw the dinghy rope out to her. She was too far out in the water and I wasn't such a great aim either. And I'd heard far too many stories of someone jumping in the sea as a rescuer only to drown themselves, so I wasn't about to dive into the water after her. And then I saw it – the half-chewed foam surfboard that I'd thrown up onto the rocks during one of my beachcombing sessions.

By now the dinghy had moved closer to shore, which should have made things easier, but the light was fading and all I could think of was the chunk of missing surfboard.

"Freya! I'm slipping."

"Oh, shut up," I hissed. I took off my shoes and peeled off my layers until I was just in my underwear. It was already cold and I wasn't even in the water yet.

I grabbed the surfboard under one arm and waded into the water.

"Hate. You. Hate. You. Hate. Hate. Hate," I droned.

I could see my skin was turning blue.

The waves were choppy but small and the adrenalin was helping my legs to power through the water.

"Freya!"

Even in her panicked state, Rumer managed to sound annoyed with me. I didn't bother to answer her but concentrated on kicking.

By the time I reached the dinghy my feet could no longer touch the sand. The boat swung slowly in the water and suddenly I saw Rumer's face, which was a mix of terror and anger.

"What took you so long!" she demanded.

"Why didn't you get back in the boat?" I asked.

"I couldn't," she said. "And I've lost the oars."

"Come on," I said. "Grab hold of this and we'll paddle back to shore."

"Okay," she said.

I waited a whole minute before I nudged her. "You can let go now, Rumer. Grab hold of the board."

"I know," she said.

And still she clung to the side of the boat. By now twilight had slipped into night. A rumble of thunder sounded closer than before.

"I wonder how many sharks they get around here?" I asked.

Rumer let go of the dinghy and grabbed the surfboard. I moved over to give her more space.

"Now what?" she asked.

"Now we kick," I said.

I won't bore you with how long it took us to get back. How scared I was that we might not make it to shore at all. Luckily the power was back on at Vinegar House and it shone bright like a beacon. Back on the beach I shoved my clothes on then prodded and poked Rumer to get her moving.

"I'm numb!" she whined, but began walking anyway.

She complained all the way back home. As we drew closer to the house I realised that the light was coming from the attic window, but I was too tired to wonder why someone had left a light on up there.

When we reached the house and I flicked the light switch in the kitchen, I realised that the power was still off.

* * *

I got Rumer into the kitchen then fumbled about in the dark until I found some matches and a candle. I placed the candle in a glass, lit another candle and held it up to Rumer's face.

"I want a bath," she said.

"There's a shower down here," I said. "Have a shower. It's closer—"

"I want a bath!" she repeated.

I didn't want to go to the upstairs bathroom, but I didn't want to stand there all night arguing with Rumer, either.

"Stand next to the wood stove and get warm. I'll go upstairs and run the bath."

She nodded.

I left her with one candle and took the other with me. As I left the kitchen she said, "Freya?"

"Yes?"

"I just want to say ... thanks. Thanks for saving me. And sorry about Luke. Sorry about everything. I hope you'll forgive me ..."

Of course, this didn't happen.

What she really said was, "Freya?"

"Yes?"

"Can you get me one of those pink towels? The white ones are too scratchy. I'll need two, one for my hair. And make sure you don't make the water too hot. I can always top it up once I get in."

"Rumer?" I said.

"Yes?"

215

"Shut up," I said.

Then I left.

If you ever want to mess with someone's head, it's easy. I do it to myself all the time. If I know I've left my drink bottle at home when I go out, suddenly I need a drink of water. I need it really badly. There is nothing that I can think of except that sweet water sliding down my throat.

The same goes for spooky houses.

I had managed to live at Vinegar House for around ten days without once thinking the word spooky. Now that it was just Rumer and me in the house with no electricity, the only thing I could think of was spooky. This house was spooky. It was old and spooky. When the hall clock chimed once, I jumped and sent out a little, "Eeek."

Then I felt embarrassed.

As I walked up the staircase, the candle threw monster shadows onto the wall and wind rattled the stairway windows as it gusted about the house. A loose shutter slapped the wall – *bang-bang*.

I paused at the top of the stairs. There was a noise coming from further down the hallway. It was coming from the bathroom – the sound of water splashing into the bath. The water pipes clanged as the heated water ran through them.

"Come on, stupid," I whispered loudly to myself.

I pushed open the door, which was slightly ajar.

I waved my candle about the room, but there was no one there. The curtain was drawn about the bath and although I wanted to leave then and there, I knew the taps needed turning off. Just a problem with the plumbing, I thought. Just like Mrs Skelton said. And the stupid plug that kept falling into the plughole.

I don't know how long I stood there but finally I reached out and pulled the curtain back, and just for a moment, in the dim light of the candle, I saw Rumer lying beneath the water looking up at me. But then no, not Rumer, it was her mother – the girl in the striped top. A scream caught in my throat, but as I pushed the candle closer I saw there was no body – just the sloshing of water in the cracked porcelain bath. I turned off the taps.

The bathroom door creaked, and I quickly turned, but there was no one behind me. A low growl from behind the clothes hamper turned me to stone. It was a long drawn-out sound and it definitely wasn't human.

It was like being in a nightmare where you want to run but you just can't move. And just when I thought it couldn't get any worse, the hamper shook and a large furry thing shot out from behind it.

It was one of Grandma's mangy cats.

I sat on the floor with a laugh. "Stupid cat," I said.

And that's when I heard a loud noise above me. It was the same noise I'd heard earlier. It sounded like Rumer was in the attic, though I hadn't heard her walk past the bathroom.

"Rumer!" I called out.

The noise stopped and all I could hear was the sound of a tap drip, drip, dripping into the bath.

"Rumer?"

And then something occurred to me that didn't make sense. I'd heard the same loud noise before. I'd heard it earlier when I thought Rumer was upstairs. But Rumer had been hanging onto a dinghy near Seal Rock when I'd heard first heard the noise, so it couldn't have been her.

"Rumer?" I whispered.

Then I heard the sound again.

Chapter 25

I don't know how long I stood in the bathroom, but it was long enough for Rumer to come looking for me.

"What are you doing?" she asked. "Is that bath ready or what?"

I think I've already mentioned I don't have a poker face. Well, there must have been something in my face that stopped Rumer talking and then she heard it too – the loud noise of moving furniture from the upstairs attic.

Rumer's face filled with alarm. She pushed me out into the hallway, and I followed her into the Blue Room, our candles casting long shadows that jumped about like goblins on the wall behind us. Then Rumer leaned in and whispered into my ear.

"Something's here."

I noticed she didn't say some*one*.

Lightning turned night into day for a beat. Thunder cracked loudly rattling the window and a loose shutter downstairs set up its crazy beat against the outside wall.

We listened to the sound of the floorboards as they creaked overhead. I tracked their progress from one end of the hall to the other, then heard the scrape of the attic door as it opened. I wished there was a lock on the bedroom door.

"It's coming!" I whispered.

"Murder in the Dark!" said Rumer, cryptically. Then she blew out her candle.

I felt her drop to the floor beside me and scuttle away as I blew out my own candle. I groped my way across to the window and pulled the curtains together, then I too dropped to the floor and slid into my secret spot under the low chair up against the tallboy.

And waited.

I heard the rattle of a doorknob up the hallway, then the clinking of something that may have been keys ... or chains. I imagined a chained ghost looking for revenge. I thought of the slip of paper I'd found in the tree house – *murderer* – and I began to shiver. I wondered if one of dead maids from the laundry room fire had come back to haunt us. Or the dead groomsman back for revenge.

There was a thud in the room next door then a low moan. I felt the darkness of the Blue Room push down on me. I opened my eyes to its oily blackness then closed them again at the sound of another thud. I felt the old panic of being in a confined space. A door slammed. Thunder rumbled. Then I heard the rattle of the doorknob to the Blue Room and pressed myself further into my hiding space.

I could hear loud breathing, and it wasn't mine.

There was the sound of the dresser drawers being roughly pulled out and the chink of metal. I thought of the stolen notes in my drawer in the next room. Did the ghost know about the notes? I should never have taken them. I opened my eyes and peered out from under the chair. Another flash of lightening lit the room and I watched in horror as Rumer scuttled to a different hiding place as a figure approached the wardrobe. I thought the nearly instant clap of thunder that followed masked her frightened shriek, but in the silence that followed I could hear more heavy breathing and then a grunt.

I heard footsteps leave the bedroom and the *clunk, clunk, clunk* of something being quickly dragged down the stairs.

Then someone called out, "Hello? Freya? Rumer?"

It was Luke.

I scrambled out of my hiding spot and fumbled to the hallway.

"Are we having dinner tonight or am I on rations?" he said with a grin.

I held a finger to my lips. There was the sound of something being dragged on the floor downstairs then the front door slammed.

"What—?"

"Has it gone?" Rumer asked as she crept into the hallway.

"What's going on?" asked Luke. "Who was that?"

"That," said Rumer, "was the ghost of Vinegar House."

Chapter 26

"What's going on?" Luke repeated.

"I think it was a ghost," said Rumer. "An unhappy ghost."

The door to the Blue Room slammed shut behind us.

Rumer jumped. "See!" she said.

"Just a draft," I said, hoping I was right. "I need to see the attic. I need the torch."

"Which means we all have to go," said Rumer. "I'm not sitting here without the torch. Wouldn't you rather just go downstairs and lock the doors. In case the thing comes back?"

"Good idea," I said. "You go down and lock the doors, and I'll go to the attic."

"But–"

"Luke will go with you."

I didn't stop to argue but moved along the hallway and up the stairs to the attic.

Another thing you should know about me is that sometimes when I get an idea in my head then I act on it straightaway, just so I don't have a chance to change my mind.

It wasn't until I reached the stair landing that I realised Luke and Rumer were right behind me.

"How did they unlock the door?" I said.

"Ghosts don't worry about doors," said Rumer.

"The door's open," said Luke.

The attic looked like my bedroom on a bad day – a mess. The neat tower of boxes had toppled to the floor. Old clothes and toys were thrown about in a colourful jumble. And standing in the middle of the room was the locked chest, which hadn't been opened.

Luke gave a low whistle, and Rumer picked up a few things, then put them down again. When I leaned against the floor-length mirror an idea hit me like a jolt of electricity. I knew where the key to the chest was.

"Wait here," I said, then I took the torch back to the Blue Room, grabbed the trinket box from the dressing table, and took it back to the attic.

"Don't do that again!" complained Rumer. "It's too dark!"

I pulled a small key out of the trinket box – the

same trinket box I had knocked over in the Blue Room all those years ago. I fitted it to the padlock on the trunk and the lock sprung open. I threw the lid back to reveal some old photo albums and letter bundles tied up with kitchen twine.

"Boring," said Rumer. "Shine the light over here, Freya."

"Use your phone," I said. Then I realised Rumer's phone was under water at Bluff Beach.

"Very funny," she snapped.

"Are there any other torches?" asked Luke.

We moved in a knot of three to the library where we found a torch each. I locked the front door while Rumer rolled her eyes at me and said, "As if that will keep a ghost out." Then we all returned to the attic.

While Rumer searched through the chaos, Luke went downstairs again to try the phone, and I checked out the letters from the chest

"What a mess!" said Rumer. "What was it looking for?"

"*It* was definitely human," I said. "A ghost couldn't make this mess."

"Heard of a poltergeist?" said Rumer.

"Where were you tonight?" I asked Rumer.

"You know where I was," she said. "I was hanging

onto a boat in the middle of the ocean."

"Why?" I asked.

"None of your–"

"I need you to tell me the truth," I said.

Rumer flicked a strand of hair from her face. "Why?" she said finally.

"Rumer!"

"Gerard," she said. "I was supposed to meet with Gerard. He's staying at Homsea with his parents for the holidays. We've seen each other every day since I got here. It's a secret. We promised our parents we'd take a break. They just wanted us to concentrate on school this year. Luke knows about us. He saw us one night down by the tree house."

"Gerard," I repeated. "The speedboat …" I remembered pointing out the boat to Luke when we were sitting in the tree house.

"It's his father's boat," said Rumer. "And when he didn't come this afternoon …" She shrugged. "I thought I'd take the dinghy and meet him. And then I lost an oar. And then, when I tried to get it, I fell out of the boat. You know the rest."

"But what about Luke?" I asked.

"Luke?" She laughed. "What about Luke?"

I untied a bundle of letters. The top envelope was

not addressed to anyone. It just held the distinctive letter *R* I'd come to know.

"Have you seen these before?" I asked.

Rumer took the notes from me and looked at them by the light of the torch. "Not these ones," she said after a moment. "But I have some in my bedroom. They just, kind of, arrived. They've been arriving, under my door, since last week."

"Did Luke write these?"

"Luke?" She laughed. "Luke did not write these, Freya."

"How do you know that?"

"Because I asked him. I had to know because … well … I didn't want him thinking that I was interested in him."

"Oh."

"I thought it was you," she said. "I thought you were playing a practical joke. So I didn't say anything because I didn't want you to think I cared."

"I would never do something like that," I said hotly.

She looked at me carefully. "No. No, I don't suppose you would," she said. "Then, I don't understand …"

She unfolded a letter and began to read it by torchlight, while I pulled out a photo album. The first few pages showed a happy blond baby with curls; then later photos of the baby as a toddler, school photos and finally a Rumer look-alike proudly showing off a baby bump.

"What have you found?" asked Rumer, holding out her hand for the album.

I handed it over, and she looked carefully at the photo.

"That's my mother," she said.

"Yes."

"That's me," she said, pointing to the bump. "These are her letters," she said slowly.

"But these letters are addressed to—"

"My mother's name was Rebecca," said Rumer. "My dad's name is Lawrence. R and L. I can't believe he wrote these to her. They're … they're … so … personal."

"Still no signal," announced Luke as he climbed the attic staircase.

I suddenly realised that Luke Hart had not hooked up with my cousin Rumer and my heart did a happy dance.

"The dining room's a mess. The cupboards are all open—"

"The silverware!" I said.

"You think it was a robbery?" asked Rumer.

"I wonder what else they've taken?" said Luke.

"You mean the ghost?" said Rumer.

While Luke and Rumer squabbled about the robber/ghost, I pulled out a flimsy blue envelope. Inside was a letter on tissue-thin writing paper. I held the torchlight close to shed light on the page.

Mother,

I've made an awful mistake. I know you tried to tell me – tried to stop me from leaving – but I couldn't stay. My head was so full of dark thoughts. I feel like such a failure. Rumer and Lawrence are the most important people in my life. Lawrence won't take my calls. I can't seem to get through to you on the home line. I'm coming home. I want to be there for Rumer's birthday. Can you please tell Lawrence that I love him? He must know that. Tell him to give our baby girl a kiss for me.

I'll see you soon.

Your loving daughter,

Rebecca

A wave of sadness – so fierce that I felt like falling – crashed over me.

"So why is this stuff all locked away?" asked Luke.

"Rumer," I said.

"Who knows," said Rumer with a shrug.

"Rumer! I think you should read this," I said. I held out the letter.

Rumer threw back her head and took a deep breath then she looked at me coolly. "Can we get something to eat? And I need to get out of these clothes. I'm freezing."

"Rumer!"

Luke shook his head at me, but I followed my cousin down the stairs.

"The stupid TV isn't even working, so we can't watch that. I've got some movies on my laptop," she said. "Maybe we can watch something on that after dinner –"

"Rumer!" I grabbed her arm and she swung around, the torchlight making her face look ghostly white.

"What!" she demanded.

"Don't you want to read this? It's from your mother. She says she loves you."

Rumer shrugged. "Sorry, cuz. What do you want me to say? My mum left and then she got herself killed, end of story."

Rumer got some dry clothes from her bedroom, then made me wait outside the bathroom door for her as she got changed.

"I might as well use that water," she said.

The sound of the pipes clanging as she topped up with hot water sent a shudder through me and I called out a few times to her just to hear her voice. Luke went downstairs to see what had happened to the spaghetti sauce. After ten minutes, Rumer emerged in her black T-shirt and PJ pants.

"Rumer–"

"I'm starving," she said. "Are you getting changed?"

We didn't talk about Rumer's mum for the rest of the night. We did talk about who had ransacked the house, though. Rumer finally gave up on the idea of a vengeful ghost.

"Where's Mr Chilvers?" asked Luke. "I thought he was coming back this afternoon?"

I explained the phone call from Grandma and what I thought her message had been.

"It was Mr Chilvers," said Rumer. "I told you he was creepy."

I shook my head. "That doesn't make sense."

"There was something about his eyes," continued Rumer, ignoring me. "Maybe he was an escaped criminal? Maybe he planned this all along?"

"Mr Chilvers was a farmer," I argued. "Besides, he knew we'd be here. I don't think our burglar was expecting anyone to be home."

We argued about the thief over dinner. Luke found Mrs Skelton's house keys lying near the front door, and Rumer insisted this proved that the intruder was definitely Mr Chilvers – that all the evidence pointed his way.

We checked the doors a million times to make sure they were locked, and then watched a movie on Rumer's laptop in the TV room. We went to sleep – Rumer on the couch and Luke and I on a chair each – with the fire crackling and the wind gusting rain against the windows. Deep into the night I woke to the sound of the clock chiming out the quarter hour and noticed Luke poking the fire and putting on another log of wood. I lowered my eyelids half-mast and watched as he tucked my blanket closer about me. I closed my eyes as he touched my cheek softly with his fingers and I couldn't help the smile that curved on my face. I wondered who had left the love notes under Rumer's door and why. Then I slipped back into sleep until I woke to the sound of a car horn tooting early the next morning.

Grandma Vinegar was home.

Chapter 27

Through the TV Room window I could see Grandma ordering a taxi driver to be careful with her luggage. Mr Chilvers was nowhere in sight.

"Quick!" I shook Rumer's shoulder, then Luke's, who snored in protest. "Come on, come on, Grandma Vinegar's home!"

I cleared the dishes from the coffee table and hurried into the kitchen, stacking them neatly on the sink. I grabbed the dirty spag bog saucepan and shoved it into the oven of the new stove – I'd clean it later.

The front door rattled and Grandma Vinegar called out, "Freya! Rumer!" Then I heard her say, "Where are my keys, Livinia?"

I brushed my hair with my fingers and tried to smooth down my clothes. By the time Grandma came through the front door we pretty much had things under control.

"Haven't you got appointments? Why are you home?" I babbled.

Grandma took one look at me and said, "Oh, my goodness, Freya, what has happened here?" and I realised I wasn't fooling anyone.

Mrs Skelton came through the door carrying the tapestry beauty case. "It's freezing in here," she grumbled. "What's all this mess?"

"I knew it," said Grandma, triumphantly. "I told you, Livinia. I knew I shouldn't have left the house yesterday. I could feel it in my bones … What has happened? Have you heard from Mr Chilvers? Is the power out?"

By now Luke and Rumer were standing sleepy-eyed at the TV room door. Grandma took one look at them, ordered Mrs Skelton to make a pot of tea, then ordered the rest of us back into the TV room. While Luke stoked up the fire, Rumer and I sat on the couch and Grandma prowled about the room like a nervous cat.

"I'm afraid Mr Chilvers and I have had a falling out," she said briskly. "An issue about his wages. Nothing for you to be concerned about."

Luke sat down on a chair.

"We had … words when we arrived in Port Eden. It seems Mr Chilvers was after a pay rise, although we'd already agreed I would look at a pay increase at the end of the next financial year … Then he took off with the car. I thought he may have come back here …" she said with a lift of an eyebrow. "I couldn't get a taxi back until this morning. It has cost me an absolute fortune. So, no Mr Chilvers?"

Rumer shook her heard but Luke and I looked at each other.

"There was … somebody here last night," I said with a little cough. "They ransacked the house. I'm not sure what they've taken – the silver definitely. It was too hard to check out in the dark."

"Someone … last night?" Grandma pursed her lips and her nostrils flared in anger. "You think it was Mr Chilvers? Did he hurt you? Did he–"

"We hid," said Rumer. "He just took some stuff. He went into the attic."

Grandma flinched. "As long as you're all right–"

"The trunk's open," said Rumer. "The one with all my mother's things. Why were they hidden like that?"

Mrs Skelton rattled into the room with a tray loaded with cups and spoons and a teapot. "I suppose you want me to pour it as well?" she said sourly.

"Thank you, Livinia, I think we are all in need of tea," said Grandma. "This is most upsetting."

"Grandma?" said Rumer.

Grandma moved over to the window and looked out. "I didn't hide things from you, Rumer. I just packed things away. It was a tragic loss–"

"How could you! She was *my* mother!"

"And she was *my* daughter," said Grandma fiercely. She pulled at the wrap around her shoulders and raised her chin a little. "Rebecca was *my daughter*," she said in a softer tone. "You were just an infant. Your father was out of his mind with grief when she had the accident. He begged me to clear her things away. He wanted me to burn everything. But I kept them. I thought ... in time ... I thought he might want to share those things with you. I've tried to talk to him ..." She shrugged. "He won't hear of it. He won't hear of it," she repeated.

"I suppose you'll want biscuits," said Mrs Skelton. Nobody said anything. "Well, I want a biscuit," she said. "And we should probably call the police. Has anyone checked the phone line this morning?"

I heard her grumbling as she moved out to the telephone.

"I'm making breakfast," I said, pulling Luke's arm. "And Luke's helping me."

I closed the TV room door behind us and hoped Grandma and Rumer might talk some more. I was scrambling eggs in a pan when Mrs Skelton came into the kitchen and announced the police were on their way.

"What are you doing there?" she asked.

"Making scrambled eggs," I said.

She shook her head. "I suppose you know what you're doing."

Luke was washing the dishes and she told him off for using too much dishwashing liquid.

"Has anyone fed *those* cats?" she asked.

Luke and I shook our heads and Mrs Skelton disappeared into the pantry on the search for cat food.

I stopped stirring the eggs when an idea struck me. "The love notes," I said aloud.

"What?" said Luke.

"The love notes, under Rumer's door …"

Mrs Skelton bustled out of the pantry and filled the cat's dishes with dry food.

"Do you know anything about the love notes left under Rumer's door?" I asked Mrs Skelton.

"Love notes?" said Mrs Skelton. "What are you talking about?"

"Someone's been leaving notes under Rumer's door."

Mrs Skelton shook her head then said, "Are you burning those eggs, Freya?"

"Did you slip those notes under Rumer's door, Mrs Skelton?" I asked.

"What nonsense. Love notes?" Mrs Skelton scoffed. "Are you trying to burn the bottom out of that pan?"

And with that Mrs Skelton pushed me aside and took over the cooking.

"Maybe you could do something useful. Both of you," she said, glaring at Luke. "There are still some bags on the front doorstep. And don't go touching anything else. The police will be wanting to look for clues or something. That's what they do, isn't it? I never trusted that man," I heard her say as the kitchen door closed behind me.

Out on the front doorsteps, I looked out to the sea which was more blue than grey this morning.

"Luke, I have to tell you something," I said.

Luke was holding had a suitcase in each hand as he came up the stairs and stopped a step down from me so that we were eye to eye.

"What?" he said.

"I'm not going out with anyone."

There was a moment's silence.

"You're not with Hamish Thomson?" he said.

"Definitely not," I said.

"That photo on Facebook?"

"Tell you later."

Then I reached up and kissed him – my very first kiss with Luke Hart. His lips were softer than I'd imagined. The kiss was better than I'd imagined.

"Well!" I heard Mrs Skelton behind me gasp.

And then I went back for a second kiss.

✱ ✱ ✱

The police caught Mr Chilvers sleeping in Grandma's car outside the Pig and Whistle Hotel in Port Eden later that morning. It seems he'd been at the hotel the day before bragging to anyone who'd listen that he worked at Burnside (Vinegar House's real name) and was allowed to take the Mercedes out whenever he wanted. The waitress told police that Mr Chilvers had been wearing a set of keys around his neck on a long crocheted chain. And when she asked him about the keys, he'd laughed and said he was playing a joke on someone and how they'd get a surprise when they found the keys missing. But by the next morning he was the one to get a surprise, for the keys were missing from around his neck.

Because there was one person who'd been listening to Mr Chilvers's stories that night. Someone who was very interested in what he had to say. They probably asked him where this amazing house was. He may have told them the owner was in Port Eden for a night. He obviously hadn't mentioned us though. It must have shocked the thief to discover someone was in the house. He also must have been annoyed not to find any jewellery. It seems Grandma always carried her jewellery with her in her large tapestry beauty case whenever she left the house.

Mr Chilvers was charged with stealing the Mercedes, but Grandma managed to convince the police that it was all a misunderstanding. I don't know if she fired him, but he hasn't returned to Vinegar House, making Mrs Skelton a very happy housekeeper. The police are still looking for the thief, but there haven't been any breakthroughs yet, and there's not likely to be, if you ask Mrs Skelton, which I did.

Chapter 28

I'd like to tell you that everything returned to normal after that winter at Vinegar House. And in some ways it did. But in other ways my life had changed forever. I understood the world a little better, well my bit of the world at least. After the police came and asked us questions about the robbery, I rang Suzette Crompt and explained to her exactly what had happened on the night of the party between her boyfriend and me. She thanked me for calling and said she figured it was something like that and she wasn't going out with him any more anyway. I swear that less than a minute later I had ten texts from people who had previously wanted to rip my eyeballs out and who now wanted to be my best friend. There were also texts from the friends who had been on my side all along. I didn't bother replying to any of them.

By the time I got home I found there was a new rumour doing the rounds at Homsea High. According to Facebook, Luke Hart and I were an item. Rumer had posted it on Facebook, and Isabella had responded by writing on my Facebook wall to ask about it, then everyone knew – or thought they did. Luke and I were officially talking to each other again – that was a fact. And if we'd started meeting up again at the jetty on Saturday mornings, and if he happened to hold my hand while we were sitting there waiting for our squid jigs to bob about in the water, then it was no one else's business except his and mine.

And that's all I want to say about that.

The burglary at Vinegar House caused the locals to shake their heads and mutter about the Kramer's Folly curse but then there was a break-in at Porky Sudholz's and a whole side of beef was stolen so they soon forgot about Vinegar House and began rumours about who might have taken the beef. I'm still waiting on an answer to that question. I'll get back to you as soon as I know.

Mum and Dad returned from overseas. Nanna was on the mend and Mum was happy to have had a visit with her. The Colonel seemed less grumpy than he had before, or maybe I just accepted his grumpiness better. Oscar returned from camp without any broken bones and Isabella went straight back to uni from her vacation, so we had to catch up via Skype. I was counting down the days to Holly's return but most of all I was happy to be home.

Oh, did I mention I got a job at the bakery? My name had finally risen to the top of the list that I'd been on forever (risen, hah, no pun intended) and I work Tuesdays and Thursdays and Saturday afternoons. This means I can still sleep in on Sunday mornings, so I'm happy. Oscar likes to come by and try to get free food from me, but I stopped giving him any after he started bringing around his whole class.

The thing that didn't change, well the person really, was Rumer. She is never going to be my favourite cousin. She will never be the type of person to just ring me up or text me to see how I am, and I pretty much feel the same way about her.

But we shared a moment – just before Uncle Lawrence drove her away from Vinegar House those holidays – that I will never forget.

"I need to ask you something," she said.

"Yeah?"

She leaned close to me, like she was going to give me one of her fake hugs, and said, "I've been thinking about those notes. The love notes from Dad to Mum. The ones slipped under my door."

243

"Uh-huh."

"You didn't put them there—"

"I already said, didn't I?" I pulled back a little from her.

She nodded, as if she was satisfied. "I know who did."

I smiled. "You do?"

"I think they were a sign. From my mother. I think she wanted to reach me somehow. You know. From beyond—" She waved her hand. "Well?" she said. "What do you think?"

I wasn't sure what to think. I looked into Rumer's blue eyes – the ones that had looked at me scornfully all my life – and I nodded slowly.

"I think you're right," I said.

"She's been here all along," she said, smugly. "Looking out for me."

"Rumer!" Uncle Lawrence called out as he started the car.

"Catch ya later, cuz," she said. "It's been real."

That night I asked Grandma about Rumer's mother. We were sitting in the TV room watching another old movie. Luke had already left for home before dinner – luckily it was Mr Hart who picked Luke up because it would have taken hours to get rid of Mrs Hart – and

Mrs Skelton had gone to bed early with a headache. I asked Grandma Vinegar about Rebecca straight out, though I wasn't sure if she'd tell me.

Grandma stood up and moved over to the fireplace, warming her hands.

"My daughter was suffering from postnatal depression," she said finally. "It went undiagnosed, but I believe that's what it was. She left her family for several months when Rumer was very young. But she did return home."

The fire settled in the grate.

"Rebecca came home the day before Rumer's third birthday. It was to be a surprise. She looked so ... well. So rested. She was so eager to see everyone, but especially Lawrence and Rumer. We were going to have a party here – the whole family was invited."

The fire crackled and a spark flew out onto the rug. Grandma stood on it to damp it out.

"We don't know for sure what happened, but I think she went for a swim at Bluff Beach. It had been incredibly hot for several days. The clothes she'd been wearing that day were laid out on her bed. There was nothing missing – her bag, everything, was in her room. I don't know if she had a swimming costume with her, but there was no costume in her luggage, so maybe ...

They found her sandals down on the rocks. We tried to keep everything … discreet. They searched for her along the coast, but … nothing. There was a rumour in Homsea that Rebecca had died in a car accident. I don't know where they got that idea. I didn't set them right. It really was no one's business."

I thought about the vision of Rumer I had seen in the bathtub on the night of the robbery that could just as easily have been Rebecca lying there under the water. I thought about the taps in the bathtub that would mysteriously run in the middle of the night, and the bathplug that would sometimes fall into place and allow the bath to fill. I wondered what time Rebecca went down to Bluff Beach that day before Rumer's third birthday. The time 2.47 am, bright on my mobile screen, was clear in my mind.

Grandma and I watched the end of the movie and I tried to pretend that I didn't notice her tears, which had nothing to do with what was happening on the screen.

And I tried to pretend that Grandma's story hadn't sent a shiver up my spine.

Later that night the grandfather clock from the entry hall woke me with its chiming. By the time it had finished I was totally awake, so I slipped out of bed and went into the hallway, where I noticed a faint light spilling down the attic stairs, just as I had expected. In the attic I stood for a while at the octagonal window, looking out past the bluff to the choppy waves that gleamed silver in the pale moonlight. After a while I turned to the floor-length mirror.

The mirror from the Blue Room.

Rebecca's old bedroom.

I didn't have an answer to the mystery of the shining light, the light that had led Rumer and I to safety the night before, except that it came from that mirror. I had seen the light several times over the years at Vinegar House and I wasn't sure what, or who, was responsible for it. But that night I looked deep and long into its depths and for a moment I thought I caught a flash of blond hair in the cracked corner.

"Thank you," I said.

And then I left.

I thought about the mirror for a long time after that, then I just let it be. I didn't tell anyone – not even Holly. So don't tell anyone, will you? It can be our secret.

✳ ✳ ✳

There are three things you should know about me if

we're ever going to be friends. The first thing is my name – which you already know. Isabella said that I could legally change my name when I get older, but I'm kind of used to it now and I think I might as well just keep it. Even though Luke Hart still likes to tease me about it whenever he can.

The second thing is that I don't believe in ghosts – not the scary white sheet, boogie-woogie type of ghost, anyway – although the Blue Room still makes me feel uncomfortable. But what I do believe is that if you're a girl who was born in Homsea, a girl who lives in a nothing kind of house with an ordinary kind of family, then you can't know everything about the world and that it's probably good to keep an open mind about things, just in case.

And the third thing is that I believe in karma. I should never have taken the love notes from under Rumer's door. They were never intended for me.

And I should never have run away from the crying Suzanne Crompt at Tara Wilcock's party. I should have stayed and tried to tell her exactly what happened, instead of running off into the night like a scared little mouse.

And I shouldn't get cross with the Colonel with his stomping ways …

Actually, I'm not a saint. Scrap that last thought.

Anyway, thinking about those things now, I've realised that karma is already here, slapping me in the face like one of Mrs Skelton's wet sheets, and it has arrived in the shape of Luke Hart. Luke is going to be the biggest load of payback karma that I've ever had to deal with before IN MY LIFE. He's already expecting me to do things, like making me watch him play football on weekends, or telling him that the biggest squid caught at high tide on Saturday morning is the one sitting in his bucket (when it is clearly in mine), or having to listen to his mother just about picking out our wedding invitations.

That woman should stick to singing.

The other day I had a dream that Luke and I were dancing like Fred Astaire and his girlfriend in that movie I watched with Grandma. I was wearing a long soft kind of dress and Luke was wearing a suit, and we were floating about the dance floor, somehow knowing all the right steps and keeping in time to the music while Luke sang to me …

In fact, this wasn't quite a daydream. It happened yesterday. Luke asked me if I could teach him how to dance one of those slow waltzy kind of dances because we'd both been invited to Porky Sudholz's sister's wedding, as she is his mother's cousin, once removed. We were sitting on the edge of the jetty with our squid lines in the water. The morning sun was sparkling like diamonds off the waves as I ordered Luke to stand up and hold out his arms. Then I slid in close to him, placed his right hand on my back and I held his other hand in mine. A couple of the fishermen down the jetty whistled, and I told them to shut up. Luke was embarrassed enough without that.

"Can you count to three?' I asked.

In my head I could hear the music from that old movie as we fumbled our steps at the end of the jetty and Luke sang those three little words, "One, two, three. One, two three. One, two, three." For a moment the diamonds of light reminded me of Vinegar House and I sent a silent hello to it from across the water, just in case it was watching.

There are other things you should probably know about me as well, but those are the three things that you should know for now: my name, the ghost thing and the fact that I believe in karma.

But enough about me ...

I think you've got something on the end of your line.

Acknowledgements

Love Notes from Vinegar House was developed during a Creative Time Residential Fellowship provided by the May Gibbs Children's Literature Trust. With special thanks to Elizabeth, Ian, Nan, Alle and Sally.

To Chris, Bryce and Caity – with thanks and love.

Thanks as always to friends and family who put up with my absence.

To my personal readers who took the time to read the manuscript and get back with comments – Alison, Bernie, BK, Bryce, Caitlin, Corinne, Dee, Jordan, Maddy and Sue.

To the Cranny's Lane Writing Group who not only read and encourage, but question, suggest, support and laugh in equal measure. The food is also good.

To Walker Books, thanks for the opportunity to come onboard.

To Mary, guardian of over-used words and strict

punctuation, thank you for using pencil and not red pen.

To Maryann, publisher of the black dog books imprint, my editor and friend indeed.

But mostly, and most sincerely, to black dog books who have figured largely in my life these last ten years. To Andrew Kelly, and his partner and publishing director, Maryann Ballantyne, for their amazing contribution to the Australian publishing industry during their time at black dog books. Your legacy includes a list of "discovered" authors and illustrators who continue to produce quality fiction and non-fiction for children, both in Australia and around the world. Thank you for the opportunity to hop on this crazy merry-go-round known as publishing. What an amazing ride it is.

KAREN TAYLEUR spent a large part of her teen years being spooked by things that went bump in the night.

Karen ignored the first three hours of labour with her second child by reading Peter Straub's *Ghost Story*. She has been known to cover her eyes during the scary bits at the movies. She doesn't actually believe in ghosts … but she doesn't disbelieve either. She's sitting with Freya on the fence.

ALSO BY KAREN TAYLEUR

One car.

One after-party.

Six people, six points of view.

BUT ONLY ONE
OUTCOME.

"Karen Tayleur's coming-of-age story is both
masterfully written and thoroughly gripping."

Frances Atkinson, The Age

"I felt I knew these people, and feared for them.
Karen Tayleur brilliantly captures the intensity of
the final days before ad~~ulthood.~~ OF MARY IMMACULATE

Carole Wilkinson

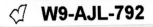

W9-AJL-792

TOMARE!

[STOP!]

You are going the wrong way!

Manga is a completely different type of reading experience.

To start at the *beginning*, go to the *end*!

That's right! Authentic manga is read the traditional Japanese way—from right to left, exactly the *opposite* of how American books are read. It's easy to follow: Just go to the other end of the book, and read each page—and each panel—from the right side to the left side, starting at the top right. Now you're experiencing manga as it was meant to be.

File 15 Stratagem

Preview of

BLOODY MONDAY

VOLUME 3

We're pleased to present you a preview from
Bloody Monday, volume 3. Please check our
website (www.kodanshacomics.com) to see when
this volume will be available!

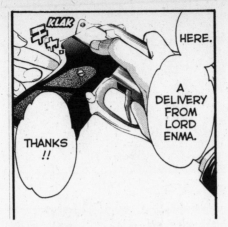

Lord Enma, page 117

Enma is the Japanese name for Yama, the Buddhist ruler of the underworld and judge of the dead. He is usually portrayed as a towering, scowling man with a red face, protruding eyes, and a black beard, wearing robes and a crown with the kanji for "king" written on it. He pops up in numerous anime and manga, sometimes as a satirical caricature, but here it is the nickname that THIRD-i members have given their fearsome Director Sonoma.

Onigiri, page 163

Onigiri are rice balls, usually wrapped in or with a rectangular piece of seaweed to provide a non-sticky surface to grip it with. They may or may not also contain one or more fillings such as pickled plum paste, bonito shavings, preserved kelp, shredded salmon, tuna salad, or shrimp tempura.

Gaijin, page 99

Gaijin, which is actually short for *gaikokujin*, is a Japanese word used to refer to foreigners. The kanji that make up the word are those for "outside", "country", and "people", or "people from outside Japan". However, in the shortened form, it can often have a negative connotation.

Kôhai, page 102

Kôhai is a Japanese word that refers to someone junior to oneself in the context of academic year or office hierarchy, with some inference of a mentor-mentee relationship. It is the opposite or counter term to *senpai*.

Kuya, page 103

Kuya is a Tagalog (Filipino) word that means "brother", specifically "older brother".

TRANSLATION NOTES

Japanese is a tricky language for most Westerners, and translation is often more art than science. For your edification and reading pleasure, here are notes on some of the places where we could have gone in a different direction with our translation of the work, or where a Japanese cultural reference is used.

"Falcon", page 37

Fujimaru's alter ego and hacker name. A phonetic pun, derived from the first syllable of his last name "Takagi"… it is only phonetic because his name uses a different kanji than that of the "taka" that means "hawk" or "falcon".

"Anko", page 42

Fujimaru's nickname for Mako. It is derived from the first syllable of her last name (Anzai) and the last syllable of her first name (Mako), but Mako's objection is likely due to the fact that "anko" is also the Japanese word for "red bean paste".

♪ BLOODY MONDAY 2 ♪.

MANY THANKS

Yamato Mitsuru   Kawabata Kunihiro
Takeda Manabu   Mattsun
Matsushita Satoshi   Hara-san
Kondo-kun

Editorial

    Sugawara-san   Sato-san   Kawakubo-san

Manga

    Ryou Ryumon X Kouji Megumi

• THANK YOU FOR READING!

HARUKA
...

CLASP

I DID FIND TWO CLUES.

THE FIRST IS AN ERASED FILE

UNFORTUNATELY, NO CRITICAL DATA WAS LEFT ON IT.

HOW-EVER-

THERE IS EVIDENCE THAT A COMPLETE PURGE WAS PERFORMED, SO I SUSPECT HE WIPED THE DRIVE TO BE SAFE.

-WHOSE NAME REMAINED IN THE CACHE.

OKITA_FILE.exe

ITS CONTENTS WERE DELETED, BUT THE FILENAME WAS STILL THERE.

TAP

IT'S LIKELY HE GAVE IT TO DEPUTY CHIEF TAKAGI, WHO THEN TOOK IT TO THE PROFESSOR.

OKITA FILE...

SECTION CHIEF OKITA...

AND WHAT'S THE SECOND CLUE?

I SEE ...

SO FROM THE LOOKS OF IT, CAPTAIN TAKAGI POSSESSES THE CONTENTS.

...

SMILE

YUP!!

'NIGHT.

KLATTER

'NIGHT!

THAN YOU HID

YEAH, SHE'S GOOD TO GO.

...THAT WE WERE ABLE TO GET HARUKA HER DIALYSIS...

AND ASADA JUST CALLED TO SAY SHE'S HOME.

I'M SO GLAD...

DON'T WORRY ABOUT IT... I WAS CONCERNED ABOUT HARUKA-CHAN TOO.

I FEEL BAD...TO HAVE MADE YOU STICK AROUND SO LATE.

BINGO.

!!

TRAFFIC LIGHTS?

YEAH... I'D HEARD THAT THERE IS A SYSTEM

THAT CAN ALLEVIATE TRAFFIC CONGESTION ACROSS TOKYO WITHOUT DECREASING THE NUMBER OF CARS ON THE ROAD...

WHAT I JUST INFILTRATED IS THE MPD'S TRAFFIC CONTROL CENTER.

-IS WHAT OVERSEES THIS SYSTEM.

THAT'S RIGHT!

AND THE TRAFFIC CONTROL CENTER-

HOW CAN HIGH SCHOOL STUDENTS BE DISCUSSING THIS...?

TO ADJUST THE TIMING AND COORDINATION OF TRAFFIC LIGHTS, RIGHT?

IT DRAWS ON AN EXTENSIVE VOLUME OF TRAFFIC DATA

File 12 A traffic jam

THAT MUCH IS CERTAIN.

THERE ARE PEOPLE OUT THERE PLOTTING SOMETHING HEINOUS-

DON'T YOU THINK... THEY'RE PLANNING TO USE THIS FOR SOMETHING?

IT'S NOT LIKE I REALLY KNOW FOR SURE, EITHER, BUT...

THAT'S FOR HQ TO DECIDE.

FUNAKI-SAN! YOU'RE GOING TO BELIEVE SUCH A TALE!?

I SEE... I'LL TAKE IT UNDER CONSIDERATION.

DETECTIVE FUNAKI! A TEACHER AT OUR SCHOOL SHOULD HAVE ALREADY DELIVERED A COPY OF THIS FILE TO THE POLICE.

THIS IS NOT SOMETHING THAT WOULD BE EASILY ACCEPTED COMING FROM A CIVILIAN...

TAKAGI-KUN.

MAY I HOLD ONTO THIS VIDEO CLIP?

HUH?

IT MAY EVEN HELP PROVIDE THE IMPETUS TO PROVE YOUR FATHER'S INNOCENCE.

IF YOU CAN ENTRUST IT TO MY CARE, I SHALL MAKE SURE THAT IT REACHES MY SUPERIORS AND GETS INVESTIGATED.

AND EVEN IT WERE, THE CHANCES THAT IT WOULD GET REPORTED UP THE RANKS ARE LOW.

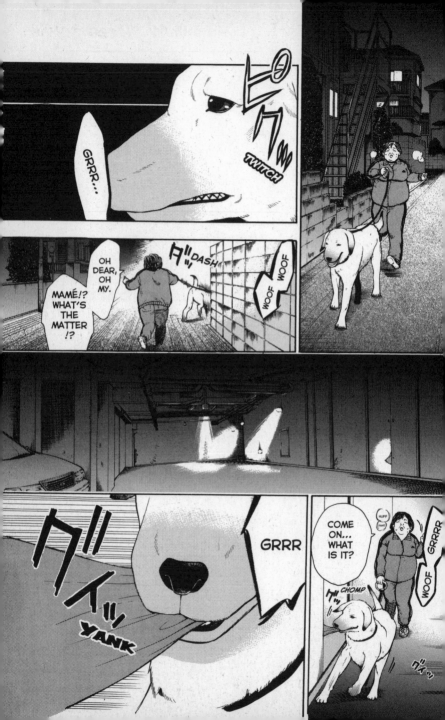

SO MY WIFE-

-HASN'T WOKEN UP YET, EITHER, HUH?

コ KLK

...I SEE.

OH, IT'S NO PROBLEM.

UM... TOMINAGA-SAN, WHAT ABOUT HARUKA'S DIALYSIS?

ほっ PHEW

THANK YOU VERY MUCH.

THEY'RE PREPPING FOR IT RIGHT NOW.

OH, AN FUJIMA-KUN.

THERE'S APPARENTLY A DETECTIVE ASKING FOR YOU AT RECEPTION.

...A DETECTIVE!?

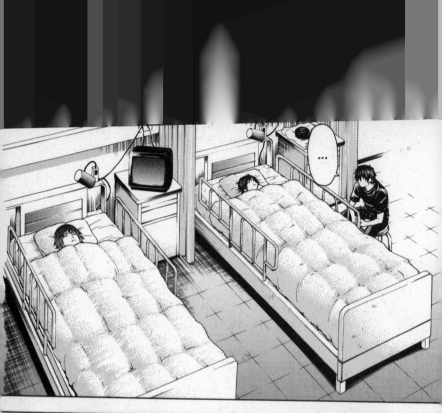

PHEW...

...

TOMORROW'S THE LONGEST SHE SHOULD GO WITHOUT IT, SO...

THAT'S A RELIEF.

FUJI MARU

TOMINAGA-SAN'S NEGOTIATING RIGHT NOW TO HAVE THE DIALYSIS PERFORMED IMMEDIATELY.

YOU'RE HAVING REGRETS NOW?

UH...

...JUST A BIT.

JUST...

SORRY TO HAVE INVOLVED YOU...

IT'S REASSURING TO HAVE YOU HERE, OTOYA.

THANKS FOR STICKING WITH ME.

KLATTER

THE GUARD WAS MAKING HIS ROUNDS, SO I COVERED FOR US.

ORIHARA-SENSEI--

WHERE HAVE YOU BEEN?

OH!

ガラララ・・
KLATTER

CHIEF KUJOU JUST CALLED TO SAY THEY RECOVERED THE TWO WHO WERE KIDNAPPED!

OH! FUJIMARU-KUN AND THE OTHERS DID IT, BY THE WAY!

AWW, PLEASE DON'T SCARE US LIKE THAT!

KLK

I DON'T KNOW HOW HE DID IT...

BUT HE SURE LOCATED HIS LITTLE SISTER MIGHTY FAST.

MY, HOW WONDERFUL!

WHAT A RELIEF.

LOOKS LIKE I OUGHT TO KEEP ALL CONTACT WITH MY 'INTEL SOURCES' HIDDEN.

ONE JUST CAN'T BE TOO CAREFUL AROUND THAT CHILD...

THAT DOESN'T MATTER, JACK DAEMON.

OUR OBJECTIVE WAS THE HACKING ITSELF, TO HAVE HIM BREAK INTO THE SUBSTATION'S SYSTEM.

THEY'RE LIKELY TO TIP OFF THE SUBSTATION... WHICH WILL LEAD TO THE PASSWORD GETTING CHANGED.

OUR PLAN IS STILL PROCEEDING ON TRACK...TOWARDS "BLOODY MONDAY".

?

GOOD WORK...

...FALCON.

File 10 An enemy close to home

BY THE TIME SOMEONE TRIES TO GAIN ACCESS AGAIN, THE PASSWORD WILL HAVE BEEN REWRITTEN.

!!

I LEFT BEHIND A LITTLE MISCHIEF-MAKING VIRUS AS A PRESENT.

RESTRICTED ACCESS ONLY
USER ID:
PASSWORD:

WHA ....!?

OF COURSE THEIR SAFETY...

IS MY NUMBER ONE CONCERN.

HOWEVER...

WHAT IF THEY HAD FOUND OUT!?

HARUKA-CHAN AND THE DOCTOR...

IT'S NOT LIKE I WASN'T UNEASY ABOUT IT!!

SHUP

...

WAIT!!

WHAE

--!!

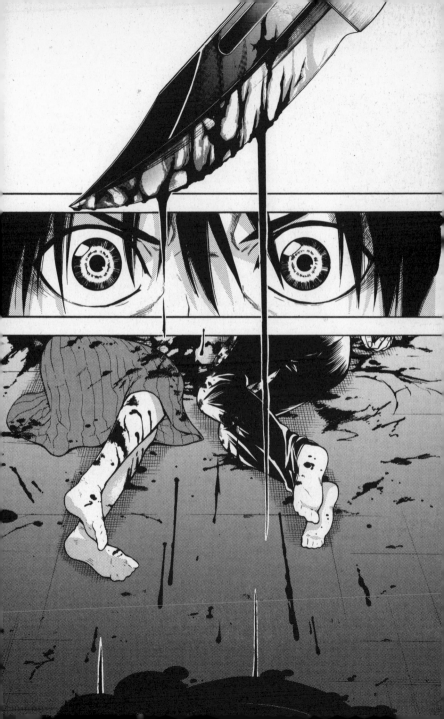

ANKO, WHAT I HAD YOU CAPTURE, USING MY ORIGINAL "SNIFFER HACKING TOOL" PROGRAM THAT I SENT YOU EARLIER,

ARE PACKETS OF THE SUBSTATION'S INTERNAL SYSTEM ACCESS DATA FILTERED ACCORDING TO CERTAIN RULES.

NOW, E-MAIL ALL OF HOSE O ME.

THIS IS THE SAME CONCEPT.

SO LONG AS THERE IS ATA COMING N AND GOING OUT, THERE ISN'T A NETWORK THAT EXISTS WHICH CAN'T BE INFILTRATED.

YOU KNOW, NO MATTER HOW HIGH-SECURITY A PRISON, A WARDEN STILL HAS TO USE A KEY TO UNLOCK AND OPEN THE DOOR WHEN ENTERING AND LEAVING.

O-OKAY ...

DON'T WORRY.

TK-TK TK-TK

FLUSH

-ANYWAY, THANKS.

...UH, COULD YOU QUIT IT WITH THE "-SAMA" ...

TH-THANK YOU SO MUCH, FALCON-SAMA!!

HERE IT COMES, HERE IT COMES!!

PRETTY PRESSIVE, ANKO! OU'RE A SAVIOR.

GOOD JOB, ANKO!

File 8　Joy and madness

Bloody Monday
- Glossary of Terms • List 4 -

Router - P13
An electronic device that relays data from one network to another.

Sniffer (a hacking tool) - P60
A program that monitors network traffic. It is also possible to use such a program to obtain user ID's and passwords by peeking at a network user's communication log.

Filtering - P60
A function that determines whether or not to permit the passage of a received packet.

Data packet - P60
In terms of computer networking, a small unit of data. By transmitting data that has been divided into a large number of small packets, it is possible to efficiently utilize network circuits.

Firewall - P75
A system designed to block infiltration of a computer network. It monitors against the interception and destruction of data and programs by unauthorized parties, and detects and cuts off fraudulent access.

Administrator Authority Authentication (Admin password) - P76
An ID or password for the administrator's use, that allows complete access to a system. With this, it is also possible to alter a system's settings.

Cache - P77
A memory function that stores data that sees a high frequency of usage.

JUST AS I THOUGHT, THE SECURITY INSIDE THE FIREWALL ISN'T THAT FORMIDABLE

...

CLIK

TK-TK-TK

WELL...
NOT
THAT ANY
SECURITY
SYSTEM-

-POSES AN
OBSTACLE
TO ME.

EH...
THERE.

POP

RENTALAND
Control
Wizard

GOOD,
HACKING
ACCOM-
PLISHED.

TK-TK

AND PULL
UP HER
LOG FROM
LAST
DECEMBER
24TH AND
25TH...

NOW I
JUST FIND
SENSEI'S
NAME AND
MEMBER
NUMBER-

RENTA LAND
www.renta-land.com

0003-0818900-9	Tachibana Kaoru
0003-0818901-1	Orihara Maya
0003-0818901-2	Matsukata Tadashi
0003-0818901-3	Tatsumiya Ran

WHICH
MEANS HER
ALIBI CHECKS
OUT... BUT
WAIT A SEC...
SOMEONE
ELSE COULD
HAVE MADE
THAT
TRANSACTION
FOR HER.

ORIHARA-
SENSEI'S
RENTAL
RECORD
SHOWS HER
BORROWING A
VIDEO AT
10:25PM ON
THE 24TH AND
RETURNING IT
AT 9:47PM ON
THE 25TH...

BINGO
!

POP

POP

12/25	[In] PM 9:47	
12/24	[Out] PM 10:25	
12/3	[In] AM 10:00	
11/26	[In] AM 10:32	Shirokujich
11/26	[In] AM 10:32	Gucci wo ki
11/26	[In] AM 10:32	Tororo

Contents

Jack Daemon
Hitman.

K

Orihara Maya
A terrorist who undertakes the "Bloody Monday" virus plot upon 'K's orders. She infiltrates Mishiro Academy in the guise of an instructor.

'K'
The mysterious individual who commands the terrorists.

Shikimura Sousuke
Ryunosuke's old college classmate. Is asked by Ryunosuke to analyze the data received from Okita.

THIRD-i

Funaki Kansuke
Member of the Metropolitan Police Department, Criminal Investigations Division 1. Heads the investigation into the incident involving Ryunosuke.

Takagi Ryunosuke
Fujimaru's father and deputy chief of the Public Security Intelligence Agency, First Intelligence Department, Third Division (a.k.a. "THIRD-i"). Framed for murder, he is currently on the run.

Hosho Sayuri
A member of THIRD-i who is asked by Ryunosuke to guard Fujimaru and Haruk

Okita Kouichi
Division Chief of THIRD-i, but is killed immediately after handing Ryunosuke certain materials.

Summary of the story through the previous volume

A Russian intelligence operative is murdered in Japan. Known connections to that incident are a woman, Maya, and a virus-based terrorist plot, "Bloody Monday"..
Super hacker Takagi Fujimaru sets out to shed light on this incident upon the request of the Public Security Intelligence Agency, where his father Ryunosuke works. As the analysis proceeds, Ryunosuke is framed for murder and is forced to go on the run. Then, based on images from the file that holds the key to this incident, Fujimaru's suspicions turn towards Orihara Maya, an instructor at his school...!!

BLOODY MONDAY
Character Introductions

Takagi Fujimaru
A second year senior high school student attending Mishiro Academy Senior High, and a genius hacker. Gets dragged into the incident while analyzing a certain file for the Public Security Intelligence Agency.

Kujou Otoya
Mishiro Academy Senior High third year student and school newspaper chief. A childhood friend of Fujimaru's.

Anzai Mako
Mishiro Academy Senior High first year student and school newspaper staff member.

Tachikawa Hidé
Mishiro Academy Senior High second year student and school newspaper staff member.

Takagi Haruka
Fujimaru's little sister and Mishiro Academy Middle School third year student.

Asada Aoi
Mishiro Academy Senior High second year student and school newspaper vice-chief. A childhood friend of Fujimaru's.

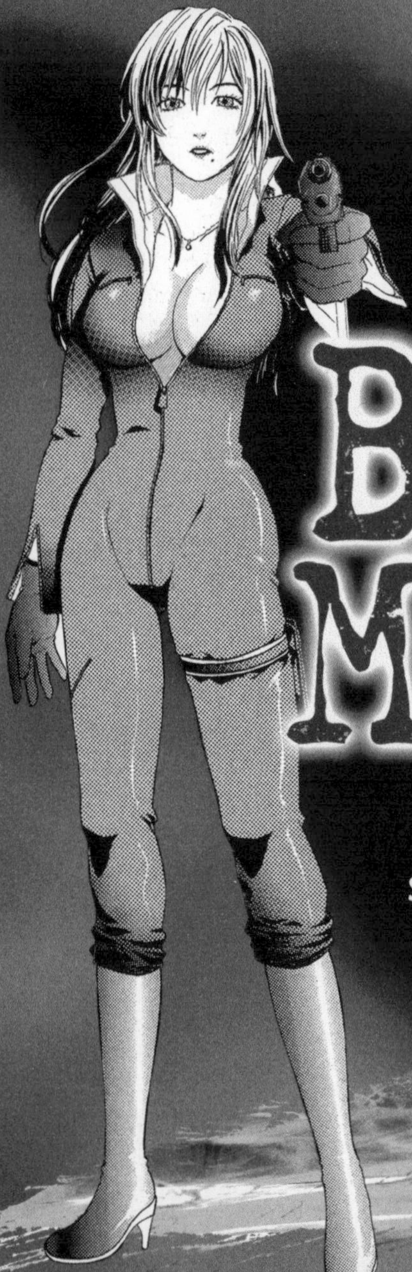

BLOODY MONDAY

VOLUME 2

Story by Ryou Ryumon
Art by Kouji Megumi

-chan: This is used to express endearment, mostly toward girls. It is also used for little boys, pets, and even among lovers. It gives a sense of childish cuteness.

Bozu: This is an informal way to refer to a boy, similar to the English terms "kid" and "squirt."

Sempai/
Senpai: This title suggests that the addressee is one's senior in a group or organization. It is most often used in a school setting, where underclassmen refer to their upperclassmen as "sempai." It can also be used in the workplace, such as when a newer employee addresses an employee who has seniority in the company.

Kohai: This is the opposite of "sempai" and is used toward underclassmen in school or newcomers in the workplace. It connotes that the addressee is of a lower station.

Sensei: Literally meaning "one who has come before," this title is used for teachers, doctors, or masters of any profession or art.

-[blank]: This is usually forgotten in these lists, but it is perhaps the most significant difference between Japanese and English. The lack of honorific means that the speaker has permission to address the person in a very intimate way. Usually, only family, spouses, or very close friends have this kind of permission. Known as yobisute, it can be gratifying when someone who has earned the intimacy starts to call one by one's name without an honorific. But when that intimacy hasn't been earned, it can be very insulting.

HONORIFICS EXPLAINED

Throughout the Kodansha Comics books, you will find Japanese honorifics left intact in the translations. For those not familiar with how the Japanese use honorifics and, more important, how they differ from American honorifics, we present this brief overview.

Politeness has always been a critical facet of Japanese culture. Ever since the feudal era, when Japan was a highly stratified society, use of honorifics—which can be defined as polite speech that indicates relationship or status—has played an essential role in the Japanese language. When addressing someone in Japanese, an honorific usually takes the form of a suffix attached to one's name (example: "Asuna-san"), is used as a title at the end of one's name, or appears in place of the name itself (example: "Negi-sensei," or simply "Sensei!").

Honorifics can be expressions of respect or endearment. In the context of manga and anime, honorifics give insight into the nature of the relationship between characters. Many English translations leave out these important honorifics and therefore distort the feel of the original Japanese. Because Japanese honorifics contain nuances that English honorifics lack, it is our policy at Kodansha Comics not to translate them. Here, instead, is a guide to some of the honorifics you may encounter in Kodansha Comics.

-san: This is the most common honorific and is equivalent to Mr., Miss, Ms., or Mrs. It is the all-purpose honorific and can be used in any situation where politeness is required.

-sama: This is one level higher than "-san" and is used to confer great respect.

-dono: This comes from the word "tono," which means "lord." It is an even higher level than "-sama" and confers utmost respect.

-kun: This suffix is used at the end of boys' names to express familiarity or endearment. It is also sometimes used by men among friends, or when addressing someone younger or of a lower station.

Authors' Notes

It is said that it is possible for a hacker to break into and take control of an Apple iPhone. Consumer electronics such as internet-connected televisions, video recording devices, and ame consoles, are increasingly popular, but it is theoretically possible for any information system connected to the internet to be hacked. Well, I suppose there aren't any hackers itching to break into an internet-connected refrigerator, though.

~Ryumon

I had my brain analyzed at a website called "Nônai (Brain) Maker". It showed that my private aspect was full of worry, and my work aspect was all clotted with erotic thoughts (my frontal lobe was comprised of cats). I couldn't have asked for a better analysis... although I would have liked dogs and other small animals, too.

~Megumi

CONTENTS